A NOVEL BASED ON THE LIFE OF

FILIPPO MAZZEI

AMERICA'S FORGOTTEN
FOUNDING FATHER

Rosanne Welch, PhD

THE **M**
MENTORIS
PROJECT

America's Forgotten Founding Father is a work of fiction. Some incidents, dialogue, and characters are products of the author's imagination and are not to be construed as real. Where real-life historical figures appear, the situations, incidents, and dialogue concerning those persons are based on or inspired by actual events. In all other respects, any resemblance to actual persons, living or dead, events, or locales is entirely coincidental.

Barbera Foundation, Inc.
P.O. Box 1019
Temple City, CA 91780

Copyright © 2017 Barbera Foundation, Inc.
Cover photo: Jacques-Louis David (1790–1791); Musée du Louvre; Painting—
    oil on canvas
Cover design: Suzanne Turpin

More information at www.mentorisproject.org

ISBN: 978-1-947431-07-2

Library of Congress Control Number: 2017959974

All net proceeds from the sale of this book will be donated to Barbera Foundation, Inc. whose mission is to support educational initiatives that foster an appreciation of history and culture to encourage and inspire young people to create a stronger future.

The Mentoris Project is a series of novels and biographies about the lives of great men and women who have changed history through their contributions as scientists, inventors, explorers, thinkers, and creators. The Barbera Foundation sponsors this series in the hope that, like a mentor, each book will inspire the reader to discover how she or he can make a positive contribution to society.

Contents

"In all circumstances I have acted in the same manner, and my behavior has been attributed more to modesty than to sound policy. I have never wished anyone to ask 'Why is Mazzei here?' but rather 'Why is Mazzei not here?'"

—Filippo Mazzei

"He was of solid worth; honest, able, zealous in sound principles moral and political, constant in friendship, and punctual in all his undertakings. He was greatly esteemed in this country."

—Thomas Jefferson

"The great doctrine 'All men are created equal,' incorporated into the Declaration of Independence by Thomas Jefferson, was paraphrased from the writing of Philip Mazzei, an Italian-born patriot and pamphleteer, who was a close friend of Jefferson… This phrase appears in Italian in Mazzei's own hand, written in Italian, several years prior to the writing of the Declaration of Independence. Mazzei and Jefferson often exchanged ideas about true liberty and freedom. No one man can take complete credit for the ideals of American democracy."

—John F. Kennedy, *A Nation of Immigrants*

Foreword

First and foremost, Mentor was a person. We tend to think of the word *mentor* as a noun (a mentor) or a verb (to mentor), but there is a very human dimension embedded in the term. Mentor appears in Homer's *Odyssey* as the old friend entrusted to care for Odysseus's household and his son Telemachus during the Trojan War. When years pass and Telemachus sets out to search for his missing father, the goddess Athena assumes the form of Mentor to accompany him. The human being welcomes a human form for counsel. From its very origins, becoming a mentor is a transcendent act; it carries with it something of the holy.

The Mentoris Project sets out on an Athena-like mission: We hope the books that form this series will be an inspiration to all those who are seekers, to those of the twenty-first century who are on their own odysseys, trying to find enduring principles that will guide them to a spiritual home. The stories that comprise the series are all deeply human. These books dramatize the lives of great men and women whose stories bridge the ancient and the modern, taking many forms, just as Athena did, but always holding up a light for those living today.

Whether in novel form or traditional biography, these books plumb the individual characters of our heroes' journeys. The power of storytelling has always been to envelop the reader in a vivid and continuous dream, and to forge a link with the subject. Our goal is for that link to guide the reader home with a new inspiration.

What is a mentor? A guide, a moral compass, an inspiration. A friend who points you toward true north. We hope that the Mentoris Project will become that friend, and it will help us all transcend our daily lives with something that can only be called holy.

—Robert J. Barbera, President, Barbera Foundation
—Ken LaZebnik, Founding Editor, The Mentoris Project

Chapter One

FAMILY FIRST AND FOREMOST

"Hail Mary, full of grace."

Elisabetta Mazzei's hoarse, dry throat repeated the opening line to that sacred prayer to the most sacred of all mothers over and over again. On the verge of childbirth, she was attended by her sister-in-law, Caterina, who joined her in prayer: "The Lord is with thee. Blessed art thou among women, and blessed is the fruit of thy womb, Jesus."

Elisabetta fell back on the very thin, straw-stuffed mattress. With force she rose up and began again between her pains. "Hail Mary—"

"Stop! Please," Caterina blurted out. "I can't bear to hear it again. Listen to the children. They are serenading your new child...music at birth promises a life of love and fortune."

"They are serenading Mary's child," said Elisabetta. Her eyes brightened at the sound of her favorite son, Jacopo, whose strong voice rose from the other room in her favorite Christmas carol:

Tu scendi dalle stele, O Re del Cielo
(You come down from the stars, oh King of Heaven)

E vieni in una grotto al freddo al gelo.
(And come into a cave in cold and frost.)

Slowly, the thinner, reedier voice of her second son, Giuseppe, joined in:

E vieni in una grotto al freddo al gelo.
(And come into a cave in cold and frost.)
O Bambino, mio Divino, Io ti vedo qui a tremar.
(Sweet child, my divine, I see you tremble.)

Then Elisabetta and Caterina joined in:

O Dio Beato! Ah, quanto ti costò l'avermi amato.
(Oh Blessed God! Oh, how much it cost you to have loved me.)
Ah, quanto ti costò, l'avermi amato.
(Oh, how much it cost you, I loved you.)

As the song faded, Elisabetta felt one last labor pain and lost consciousness. When she awoke, Caterina was placing the newborn in the arms of Elisabetta's husband, Domenico, as he, Jacopo, Giuseppe, and Domenico's parents entered the small bedroom together. It was December 25, 1730.

"What's his name?" young Giuseppe blurted out.

Nonno Giuseppe smiled broadly as he always did, and tousled the curly black hair of his outspoken grandson, who beamed. "You have already given my name to one son," he said to his daughter-in-law.

So far Elisabetta had followed the Italian tradition of passing down names from generation to generation, but a third son offered an opportunity to choose a name to her liking. Before she could catch her breath to respond, Domenico spoke.

"Domenico."

Elisabetta had never liked her husband's name, but had never told him so, and she wasn't sure how to change Domenico's mind when it was made up.

But Nonno Giuseppe had no such apprehension. "No," he said forcefully, "this is Christmas and this child is a gift from God, third in line to a fine family. He has followed Jesus into this world today, so he shall be named for the apostle who followed Jesus first, Filippo."

Because Jacopo, the eldest child, loved showing off, and hated to see his mother interested in anyone but him, he began to recite. "Filippo, third son of King Amyntas III, was father of Alexander the Great."

Elisabetta closed her eyes, immensely enjoying the sound of her favored son's voice. The seven-year-old noticed this favor, as always, and continued, though his memory began to fail him. "Filippo reformed his army...and was assassinated by his own bodyguard."

Domenico could not defy his father, for he was not in such a habit. Instead, he mumbled, "We've already promised your namesake to the church when he's old enough. I don't need two priests in the family."

Finally, Nonna Maddelena found her moment. She took the child from her son's arms and cradled him in her own. "No," she said, "Jacopo will belong to the business, Giuseppe will belong to the church, and this one, this Filippo, he will finally be our scholar."

"But *I* want to be the scholar..." Jacopo began.

"Enough," Domenico brusquely quieted his son. "Do not disrespect your *nonna*. You will run my business. Filippo—"

"Filippo will be our scholar," Nonna confirmed.

No one standing in the room that day could imagine how true that prediction would prove to be, least of all the young infant listening gently as Caterina, always the mediator, led the family in the hymn:

O Dio Beato! Ah, quanto ti costò l'avermi amato.
(Oh Blessed God! Oh, how much it cost you to have loved me.)
Ah, quanto ti costò, l'avermi amato.
(Oh, how much it cost you, I loved you.)

Six years later, Filippo found himself living his nonna's dream, sitting in a classroom in Prato, about five miles to the north of his hometown of Poggio a Caiano, and roughly ten miles from the great Renaissance city of Florence. All three cities lay within the Grand Duchy of Tuscany, as that section of Italy was known before the unification of 1870. Though his nonna's word "scholar" rang in his ears, he wasn't so sure he wouldn't rather be Jacopo, apprenticed to their father's timber mills and riding the horse to visit clients all day, or Giuseppe, reading the Bible for hours in preparation for entering the seminary. After all, the Bible was full of stories about miracles. Filippo's studies were full of far too many dead war heroes and daily recitations of Latin and Greek conjugations. Luckily, even at the age of six, Filippo had a facility for language that would serve him well across all his life's travels.

"To travel. *Adiciō, adicis, adicit, adicimus, adicitis, adiciunt.* To travel," Filippo chanted mindlessly while Professor Rosati listened for mistakes.

Filippo had a restless spirit. He questioned everything and always wanted to know why unfairness and injustice seemed to thrive in the world. Often, while he recited by rote, the young boy's mind wandered off on such questions. Other days he dreamed of the far-off places he would someday see, like Florence, which was more than ten whole miles away. Or England. Or India, with its spices and the Taj Mahal he had seen drawings of in Professor Rosati's books. Or that fantasy land across the ocean, discovered by an Italian over a hundred and forty years earlier.

When he wasn't daydreaming about a faraway land, Filippo missed sitting inside by the fire at home on a rainy day, watching Aunt Caterina and Mama help Nonna make the daily pasta. The ladies in his family smiled when they were working together, much more than when Papa came home after a long day at work. Filippo missed the many cousins who played in the streets with him all day. He also missed his new little sister, Vittoria. But mostly he missed sitting in his *nonno's* store, watching him comfort those who could not yet pay their bill. His mind flew back to the time one woman came into the store crying, but left smiling and carrying a loaf of bread.

"*Che è un successo,*" Nonno said as he slapped Filippo on the back in pride.

"But she didn't pay her bill," the young boy said tentatively, never wanting to question his precious grandfather. "And you still gave her the bread Nonna baked. How is that a success?"

"God will smile on me when we meet in *Paradiso*," Nonno said, and quoted his favorite Bible verse: "For I was hungry and you gave me to eat, I was thirsty and you gave me to drink."

Filippo joined in: "I was a stranger and you invited me in."

"Let this be your guide in life, for as you invite in strangers, so strangers shall invite you. But do not do these things in hope of earthly rewards," Nonno cautioned him, then added, "Do not be like Jacopo. I see when he behaves well it is only for show. He will see. Someday, all of this will go to the brother who earns it, not merely he who was born first."

"I won't be like Jacopo, Nonno. I'd rather be like you." The boy beamed when he imagined being anywhere near as good as his grandfather. He was too young to understand the importance of inheriting his grandfather's lands and money; he only wanted to be loved by such a good and gracious man.

With the dream of demonstrating benevolence in his mind, Filippo turned to the next customer who entered the store with a smile on his face, a welcome in his voice, and another free loaf of bread in his hands. "*Buongiorno.* May I help you?"

Smack! The intruder punched Filippo in the face, pushed Nonno to the ground, and grabbed the pouch full of coins from the day's transactions. Filippo scrambled to his feet, but the intruder knocked him down again as he ran out. Filippo moved to run after him, but Nonno's voice held him back.

"No!" Nonno insisted. "Leave it be. Your life is more precious than money."

Filippo wavered between listening to his grandfather and running after the robber, but in the end Nonno won. Filippo ran to him to see if he was all right.

"I'm fine," Nonno promised. "And so are we all." He pulled a handful of coins out of his pants pocket. "Always keep savings aside, keep it safe, for later." Then he handed Filippo one coin of each of the Tuscan denominations. "Know these things so you won't ever be cheated."

"I won't ever be cheated, Nonno," the boy promised.

Smack! The professor's stick caught Filippo in the shins and shattered his beautiful reverie. "I said it was time to turn to literature. What are the three parts of Dante's *Divine Comedy*?"

Quickly, Filippo changed gears. "Inferno, Paradiso, and…" he stumbled.

"Purgatorio before Paradiso," the professor finished with another flourish of the stick. "Giuseppe never forgot Purgatorio, which is why he will make an excellent priest. Neither did Jacopo, who is on his way to being the true scholar of your family. What a waste to see him in business. But what will you be, my young charge, if you cannot focus better than your brothers?"

Filippo wondered this himself as he turned to his reading work. In all his years of studying, what Filippo never understood was the way Jacopo made people think he was good when the family knew his frequent unkindness. Whenever he thought of his older brother nowadays it was of the time Mama sided with Jacopo over Filippo despite Nonno's best efforts to change her mind. Filippo had given Nonno's Tuscan coins to his mother for safekeeping. Some days later, he wanted to use one of them to buy a treat.

"Mama! Mama!" he had shouted as he ran into her arms, which were covered in flour as Elisabetta and Nonna had been kneading more bread to offer the poor. In the corner, Jacopo stoked the fire. "May I have one of my coins?" asked Filippo. "I'm going to buy—"

"Those are my coins," Jacopo insisted.

"You lie! Nonno gave them to me," argued Filippo from the comfort of his mother's arms.

"Don't disrespect your older brother, Filippo," Mama said as Jacopo took shelter under her other arm. She absentmindedly tousled Jacopo's flyaway hair and murmured *Cuore mio*—"my heart"—to him out of habit.

That endearment gave Jacopo the support he expected. "He gave them to you to bring to me," Jacopo said sadly to his mother. Then he shouted at Filippo, "You lie!"

"All we have to do is ask Nonno," Filippo said.

"That would mean you think your older brother is lying. We can't have love in this family if we treat each other with such disrespect," Mama continued while Filippo squirmed.

"But you always take Jacopo's side," Filippo said as gently as he could. "Always."

"And you always rush to conclusions, you rush everywhere, my little Fastidio."

Mama handed the coins to Jacopo, who knew enough to stop talking when he was on the winning end of the discussion. She turned to Filippo. "This will be a lesson to you, my son."

Filippo noted that she never used the "*cuore*" endearment when speaking to him and realized that despite how hard he tried, he could never win out over Mama's favorite. Never.

When he complained to his grandfather later, the answer was simple. "It is a fact of life that a Mama will often love her firstborn son best. Perhaps because he is the one who made her Mama in the first place."

"But—" began Filippo.

"But nothing. I know, because I was the third son, too. I also know that fighting against what is true is a waste of time," Nonno said as he hugged Filippo. "But that doesn't mean you stop. It means you double your efforts because someone, someday, will see the truth in you."

School days went on with Filippo daydreaming and Professor Rosati drilling him until Jacopo moved away to live with the tutor preparing him for university and Giuseppe moved into the seminary. Then his parents brought Filippo back home to study in Poggio with a new Latin teacher. One day, quite early in the new experiment, Filippo came running to his father's timber company office.

"Papa! Papa!" Filippo cried as he ran around looking for his father among the many workers. He crashed right into his uncle, Father Mazzei, and became entangled in the older man's long black cassock.

"What is it, Filippo? What can have you away from your studies so soon in the day?" Father Mazzei asked gently.

"I threw a stone at my professor," Filippo confessed, his words running together as he offered his swollen arm to his uncle. "But he broke a chair over my arm! For nothing!"

His uncle examined the large red welt and felt gingerly around the wrist and elbow bones as Domenico approached from his office. "What now?" he asked.

Filippo launched into a long explanation of how his teacher hit him often, even when Filippo knew he had given the correct answer. But his father cut him off.

"You will never argue with a teacher," Domenico said brusquely. "What do I pay them for?"

Filippo's heart fell. Would neither of his parents ever believe him? "I had all my conjugations correct. I did. I know I did." He began reciting, but his father cut him off again.

"Who is the teacher and who is the student?" Domenico demanded, ready to strike the boy himself.

Father Mazzei grabbed his brother's arm before it contacted Filippo's face. "That teacher is a miserable idiot," he said matter-of-factly. Then he gently added, "Today of all days, let the child win." The two men exchanged a sad look that was not lost on the young boy.

"Why today?" Filippo asked. Neither man would answer him.

It wasn't until Filippo returned home that day that his little sister, Vittoria, told him the terrible story of Giuseppe's first day at the Capuchin monastery. She told the story dramatically, as befitted the youngest and only girl among a set of brothers.

"Uncle—who traveled with Giuseppe, you know—told Mama and Papa that the first thing the monks did was shave his head," Vittoria began when the two were alone. "Imagine, all his beautiful curls dropped to the floor like so much straw for horses. I can't picture Giuseppe without his beautiful, beautiful hair. Uncle says they do that to all the novitiates so they won't be too prideful. Then they took all his clothes—his beautiful shirt, you know the one Mama let me sew the sleeves on? And they dressed him in sacks tied with rope."

Filippo's eyes began to tear up at the thought of his handsome brother being disfigured in such a manner. Vittoria noticed.

"He cried, too, Uncle said!" she claimed in awe. "Uncle said even *he* cried, so it's okay if boys do."

Filippo did more than cry. He wept most of the night over this first experience of loss, but he also began to formulate a plan—the kind of plan that makes sense to a seven-year-old.

The next morning, Domenico announced without emotion that Filippo would be returning to Prato and to his studies with Professor Rosati at the end of the week. Filippo knew he had to work fast, to live up to his nickname "Fastidio," if he were to succeed. The morning of his departure he made much of missing them all as he walked down the street carrying his satchel. Instead of turning toward Prato, however, he walked the five miles to the monastery and presented himself as another novitiate, determined to live again with his beloved brother. Though Vittoria's story about the monks made them seem mean and cruel, the very head of the order welcomed Filippo and offered him supper after his long walk. No one brought him to Giuseppe, however, and when his uncle stormed into the dining hall, Filippo learned why.

"You already have the child we've promised the church," Father Mazzei said, standing toe to toe with the Capuchin. "This one comes back with me."

"But I want to stay with Giuseppe!" cried Filippo.

"Giuseppe belongs here," Father Mazzei said. "You belong in school. That is the way of the world. Accept it or you will never survive." His uncle dragged him out of the monastery as the Capuchin looked on in disapproval.

A week later Filippo sat again before Professor Rosati, now resigned to never seeing his brother again and sure this was the worst experience of his young life. Meanwhile, there were more unpleasantries to endure. The students spent one full day on their knees in prayer upon hearing that Gian Gastone, son of Cosimo III, the last male heir to the Medici Grand Ducal line, had died. As a seven-year-old, Filippo knew nothing of the political machinations of the Medici family, only that a leader had died and rosaries had to be said for his soul, one Hail Mary after another, over and over, all morning long. Such rituals were deeply difficult for young boys to practice since the only movement allowed was the fingering of the beads of their rosaries. Teachers would slap a switch across the boys' bottoms if they were seen fidgeting, so Filippo fell back on daydreaming to pass the time.

A few weeks later, one of Nonno's best customers, a farmer from the outskirts of Poggio, arrived at Professor Rosati's home in the middle of a lesson on handwriting. Filippo had been rewriting the year, 1737, over and over again, trying hard to make the 7s match. The farmer handed a letter to the professor, but Filippo didn't need to be told what it said. He took one look at the men's faces as his teacher read the missive, dropped his quill pen, and ran toward home.

Within days he found himself standing beside the newly dug grave of his beloved Nonno, felled by a stroke. His mother stood in the parish churchyard, holding hands with Domenico and Jacopo. Aunt Caterina held Filippo's hand as Father Mazzei read the scripture and the sons of six of Nonno's friends lowered the coffin into the ground. What Filippo noticed most was not the brightness of the sun or the deep green of the trees at this time of year, but the many, many poor local peasants who stood at the grave and wept.

Who else will bake bread for them from now on? Who will help the less fortunate? Filippo wondered, but the answer came to him almost before the question left his lips.

I will.

Chapter Two

FRIENDS (AND LOVERS) AT SCHOOL

Ten years later, Filippo, serious and lean at seventeen, stood on Piazza Santa Maria Nuova in Florence, at the gates of Santa Maria Nuova Hospital, unsure whether he could even enter a place with such an imposing history. Founded in 1288 by Folco Portinari, the father of the beloved Beatrice of Dante's *Divine Comedy*, Santa Maria Nuova was also the place where Leonardo da Vinci had once been a medical intern, as Filippo was about to be. How could he even begin to walk in such shoes? It was one thing to hold in your hand a book that told the story of your hero. It was quite another to come face-to-face with the proof of his earthly existence.

He was less than fifteen miles from his parents' house, but it may as well have been 1,500, so far from home was he. It made Filippo wonder how much farther he would travel in his life. He had cried a bit at leaving home, leaving his friends and the places where he could turn any corner and remember his nonno, but now that he was here, Filippo felt exhilarated about his next stage of life. Having been turned away by the Capuchins as a child, he knew the church was not his calling, though he still felt an interest in life in the church. Was medicine his calling?

Domenico initially opposed the idea of Filippo becoming a surgeon, but seeing how much his wife adored Jacopo's intellect, he had decided it suitable for Filippo. Filippo would study medicine, hoping perhaps then Mama would love him and Jacopo equally. Remembering this motivation, he took a deep breath, switched his leather suitcase into his left hand so the right would be available for shaking hands with the new friends and teachers he was about to meet, and stepped through the gate.

Courses at Santa Maria Nuova—or "Nuova," as the students called it for expedience—often challenged, sometimes frightened, but always stimulated Filippo. Learning was not confined to the campus. Local religious leaders visited artist salons held in the homes of the Renaissance city's most esteemed intellectuals. As a student at Nuova, Filippo found himself the beneficiary of several invitations on a weekly basis.

At one such salon at the home of his new friend Raimondo Cocchi, Filippo found himself in a heated debate about purgatory and divine intervention with a vacationing lecturer from the University of Pisa, Father Crisilli. It all began with a story that had been bothering Filippo for years, ever since he first heard his nonna talk about it while baking the bread for the peasants.

"My nonna handed a loaf to one of the peasant women in my village," began Filippo, "and then she crossed herself and said a Hail Mary. When I asked why, Nonna said that the woman was a midwife and had done a blessed thing."

"What blessing can an untrained, unordained midwife provide?" Crisilli scoffed as he rubbed the wrinkles under his eyes.

"She saw the child's life was ebbing too soon and rushed him off to my uncle for baptism," Filippo explained.

"And by what magic is this uncle privileged to provide a baptism?" asked Crisilli.

"My apologies," said Filippo. "I forget, you do not know my village. My uncle is Father Mazzei of our local parish."

Crisilli seemed satisfied with this outcome. "Ah, then it is he who blessed the child so that it could reside in the house of the Lord forever. It is due to the intercession of the church, not the midwife."

"That's my question, Father Crisilli," Filippo began tentatively. From similar discussions with his uncle over the years he had learned that one must tread lightly when questioning the church. "Many, many sad children are not privy to such a fast-thinking midwife—but I cannot reconcile myself to the conception of a divine justice that would relegate some infants to eternal happiness and others to eternal suffering due to the negligence of those who happened to be around them when they were not yet capable of making such a decision for themselves."

Crisilli stiffened. "To die unbaptized is a grievous sin," he said, and Filippo nodded in agreement. "But to question such matters is also a grievous sin."

Filippo's face fell. Would no religious man manage to assuage his fears of the existence of an unjust God?

Crisilli could see the young man was not pleased with his response. He began to write out a note for Filippo. "There are people especially trained for such discussions, much more erudite than I, who handle such matters."

When the Father handed Filippo the note, the young man shuddered. "The Inquisitor? He will imprison me for my doubts when I am only trying to strengthen my faith. No, I do not wish to have anything to do with the Inquisition." Then, seeing the Father's face, Filippo tried to lighten his reaction. "You know what happened to Galileo."

"No need to be afraid. I am an honorable man, not a spy," Crisilli promised. "I have written the note in such a way that you can go quite safely and have your question answered, as you hope."

After Crisilli had left, Filippo sat over a late espresso with Raimondo, a second-year intern at Nuova whose own father, the renowned Dr. Antonio Cocchi, was also their professor of anatomy. The two young interns had been eating and studying together since the first day.

"Should I go or not?" he asked Raimondo.

"My father would say…" Raimondo began to do his very good impersonation of his father's lecturing style, though he never did it in front of his father, "'…nothing is learned if nothing is tried. Imagine—'"

At that moment Dr. Cocchi appeared in the kitchen doorway behind Raimondo and joined in on the impression: "Imagine, the first doctor who opened up a cadaver and held a human heart for the first time."

Raimondo's voice faltered as his father's grew stronger.

"Imagine. My son listens to my lectures." Dr. Cocchi smiled and tossed back the last of Raimondo's espresso. "But there will be none of us prepared to listen—or to lecture—tomorrow if we don't get some sleep tonight."

As he walked up the narrow steps to his bed for the night, Filippo wished he felt the same comfort and connection to his own father, but knew it was not to be. Nonno had been his great support, and after Nonno's death Father Mazzei tried to advise and approve as Filippo faced the move to Florence. Domenico never seemed to notice his third son, much less agree with many of his ideas. *Perhaps that is why I wonder so many things,* Filippo thought as he readied for bed.

~

Though Filippo remained uncertain about visiting the local Inquisitor, Dr. Cocchi's philosophy of trying gave him the final motivation to present Father Crisilli's note. The local Inquisitor promptly invited Filippo to a discussion over dinner at a local café. It took three such four-hour dinners across a month for Filippo to realize these meetings were not intended to assuage his doubts, but to crush them into nonexistence. Once he realized no answers were forthcoming, and worse, that such long harangues would continue across the months until Filippo declared himself doubt-free, he did exactly that. Pleased with himself, the Inquisitor then invited Filippo to be reblessed at the local church. Filippo begged off, saying he did not need such a ceremony as his faith was now completely solid, but the Inquisitor felt it was the only way to obliterate all measure of the devil's ideas. To put an end to the whole experience, Filippo finally consented to letting the Inquisitor bless him by tapping his shoulder with a religious artifact, then embrace him and send him away with a promise that they would be friends forever.

"Since then I have had no further doubts," Filippo declared to his group of friends as he regaled them with this story over a friendly card game of scopa—"friendly" being a polite word for wagering between friends. Having won ten lire the night before, Filippo had bet that much tonight, and more…to the point where he was digging into money set aside for living expenses. This time, he lost all of that, plus over fifty scudi he did not have on hand, but added to the pot with his marker.

As he handed over the money and the marker, one of the players said, "We need more than a marker to secure the debt."

Filippo stuck his hand in his vest pocket, fingering the coins his nonno had given him the day of the robbery so long ago, the ones he had begged his mother to give him as a gift when he had graduated. They were the only monies left to him. Filippo pulled them out of his pocket and suggested a deal. "For me, and for the honor of our friendship, may you hold these coins for twenty days, allowing me the chance to redeem them."

The new player wasn't sure, but then Filippo's friend Giuseppe Michelini stepped forward. "You can trust this gentleman," Giuseppe promised. "I trust him so well that I promise to cover his losses if he does not."

This assuaged the new player and he agreed to the twenty-day moratorium. Meanwhile, Filippo worried about how exactly he would raise enough to pay his debt and keep himself in food and shelter until his father's next tuition monies arrived. He could not ask his nonna or his mother, for they would surely tell Papa of this disgrace. Whom could Filippo trust to keep such a secret? Not Jacopo, who would use it as another way to denigrate Filippo among their village friends. He knew he could trust his beloved brother Giuseppe, but he had taken a vow of poverty, so he would have no money to send. Aunt Caterina! He saw her happy face in his mind and quickly dashed off a letter begging for a loan of the necessary funds and threatening to "run away to distant lands" if he didn't receive the funds *presto,* and asking her not to mention this event to Domenico. Three days later, a local Poggio farmer arrived at Nuova with a small bag full of coins and a response from Aunt Caterina.

Cara Filippo,

I apologize it took time, but without asking your father it took me a few days to collect it all. You are obliged to thank Father Mazzei for contributing enough to complete the amount. And

*I would be obliged if you never fell into this situation again,
but if you do, don't hesitate to turn to me.*
Love, Zia Caterina.

Filippo kissed the bag of money, nearly kissed the farmer
who brought it, and ran back to his rooms.

He considered risking a little of this newfound bounty in
order to win a larger sum to pay Aunt Caterina back. The words
of Dr. Cocchi came to mind: "Nothing is learned if nothing is
tried." Did that mean he ought to try one more time to make
the money back? Then the promise he made to his nonno rang
in his ears: "I won't ever be cheated." While his friends did not
cheat him in playing the game, Filippo realized gambling itself
was a cheat. It promised you joy, but there was no security in
that promise. There and then, he promised himself he would
never gamble again, and he never did, at least not with money.
Life would offer him other kinds of gambles—over the places he
traveled, the causes he supported, and the women he loved, one
of whom he was just about to meet.

On a short visit home, Filippo stood with his sixteen-year-old
sister, Vittoria, outside their nonno's shop, which she now ran.
A young lady burst into their conversation, giving Vittoria an
exuberant embrace.

"Vita!" the young lady shouted with glee.

"Sandrina!" Vittoria returned the warm-hearted hug.

"Sandrina?" asked Filippo in shock. Could this elegant
young woman be the little girl, the daughter of his beloved
godparents, who had played street games and sung with him in
church all those years ago?

"Of course this is Sandrina," said Vittoria with a smile, seeing the adoration on her brother's face.

"You don't recognize me," Sandrina teased, with a pronounced pout.

"Well, yes," stumbled Filippo. "Of course, I see now in your eyes. How are my godparents?" he asked, both to be respectful and to divert attention from his mistake.

"They are well," Sandrina answered and then used his feint to her own advantage. "Will you be visiting us while you're home?"

"It would be rude not to," Vittoria nudged.

"It would be rude not to," Filippo agreed.

From that day, he and Sandrina were inseparable until the time for Filippo to return to his studies. The night before he left, he was as honest as he could be with her.

"If I were in a position to take a wife," Filippo began, "I would prefer you above all women I have known. But I am still only a student, with no independent means of support."

"I understand your circumstances," Sandrina replied, but then hesitated. There was more to say and she was unsure of how to say it. "But I don't know if you will understand mine. I need to be honest, though I fear it will lose your affection."

"Never, my love."

"Another promised his love and loyalty to me…and I believed his sincerity and so I gave him certain privileges—"

"I understand, my love," Filippo interrupted to keep her from voicing her regret fully. "And I love you more. If you will wait for me to finish school—"

"I will wait forever," she vowed.

From that point on, Filippo determined to study harder and longer in order to graduate sooner and claim a position at the hospital that would allow him to marry Sandrina. Luckily, his godfather found reason to do work in Florence on several occasions across the next few months and each time he brought Sandrina. The two young lovers walked from one artwork to another in the city, often stopping off at the nearby church of Santa Margherita de' Cerchi to pray at the grave of Folco Portinari. Filippo told Sandrina how students often went there to pray to the founder of their hospital for help on their exams. She was more interested in Portinari's connection as the father to Dante's real life Beatrice.

"Imagine, crawling through hell on her word," Sandrina thought out loud.

"Who says I wouldn't do that for you?" Filippo teased as they exited the churchyard.

On her frequent trips to Florence with her father, Sandrina and Filippo would sit outside at a café across the street from Santa Maria Nuova and grow even closer as they debated the day's news over coffee.

"It is odd that I, the male, should be teaching you, the female, that you have every right to study what you wish," Filippo found himself insisting to Sandrina on one such visit. He had been regaling her with the story of two married couples from the University of Bologna whom he had been privileged to meet as they guest-lectured at Nuova. One of the couples, professor Giovanni Manzolini and Anna Morandi Manzolini, were well-known makers of wax anatomical models, used for medical studies. In the other couple, Giuseppe Veratti and Laura Caterina Bassi, Bassi had earned the second doctoral degree ever granted to a woman and became the first woman to earn a professorship from a university in Europe. Bassi brought

Newtonianism, the concept of the universe as governed by rational and understandable laws, to popularity in Italy.

"If I hadn't read that in the newspaper myself, I would not believe it," Sandrina insisted. "Not because I don't think a woman can do such a thing, but because I don't know any fathers or brothers—or husbands," she said with a wink, "who would allow their women to do so."

"The place of women in society is changing," insisted Filippo. "We can be such a couple."

"Perhaps," mused Sandrina. "Perhaps. But now I must meet Papa or we will miss our coach."

They tossed back the rest of their espressos, now cold for all the time they had spent avoiding saying goodbye, and ran to the station holding hands.

Sadly, their union was not to be. A month later Filippo contracted a malignant fever that all the ministrations of Dr. Cocchi could not abate. The young student lay in his bed in his rooms near Nuova in a haze, never sure what time of day or night it was each time he woke from his sweaty sleep. Cocchi tried everything he knew, and Filippo's friends from the hospital came by often with new ideas and new treatments. At first, the older doctor dismissed their ideas, but by the end of the week with no progress, he allowed them to attempt a few, while also writing a letter home to Domenico, telling him to come to Florence to be with his son in case the fever might take him.

Domenico arrived the next day. Luckily, the fever had broken that night with no one knowing whether to thank Cocchi or Filippo's friends and their innovative treatments, or merely the grace of God. Filippo returned home with his father to convalesce, believing it would be a chance to make public his dreams of marriage to Sandrina now that he had cheated death. Instead, Domenico came down with the same fever, and it seemed to take an even stronger hold on the older man.

Filippo, his mother, and Vittoria called Jacopo home from his position at the University of Pisa and Father Mazzei back from his work at the priory to sit at Domenico's bedside. Despite all their good wishes, Domenico died within days, surrounded by his loved ones.

His last words were a plea to Father Mazzei about his children. "They are left all alone!"

"No," promised Father Mazzei. "I will watch out for them, brother, as if they were my own. Elisabetta will never want for bread, Filippo will finish his studies, and Vittoria will be provided a dowry that the town will never forget."

With that promise in his ears, Domenico died, holding Elisabetta's hand. Hauntingly, Filippo noticed that instead of looking to Father Mazzei in her moment of need, his mother looked directly at Jacopo, who smiled oddly. Filippo worried at his brother's ability to smile in any manner at such a sad moment.

A few weeks later, as Filippo prepared to return to his studies at Nuova having buried his father and fully convalesced from his own bout with the fever, he understood his brother's smile. Rather than leave the family management to their uncle, Jacopo gave up his chair at the university to stay in Poggio. He then urged Father Mazzei to return to his duties at the priory, which the older man did, leaving Filippo and Vittoria without a supporter in town.

"What do you mean there is no money?" Filippo argued one morning at breakfast after Jacopo expressed doubts about allowing Filippo to continue at Nuova. "The timber business is thriving!"

"So Papa wanted us to believe," Jacopo began slowly. "But I have looked at the books. I have seen the debts. We will all need to contribute to its payroll or it will fail, leaving us with nothing. Your allowance for Florence must be cut."

"Fine, then," Filippo decided. "I'll take my portion of the inheritance and manage that myself."

"I discussed such a request with Uncle before he departed," said Jacopo.

"You discussed my affairs without me in the room?"

"These are delicate matters. Tradition decrees there is no split of the estate. As the eldest son, on the death of our father, it belongs to me."

"This is ancient tradition. It has no place in modern Italy," Filippo argued. "Papa spoke often of dividing among us!"

"That is easier said than done," Jacopo insisted. "We must allot for Vittoria's future dowry as that is an outstanding debt of Father's…."

"*Certo*," agreed Filippo.

"How can we know now how much she will need later?" Jacopo asked cagily.

"How do I know how much Sandrina and I will need once *we* wed?"

"Perhaps you should consider marriage now. Her dowry can assist you as you finish your studies."

"You know her father will never agree to her marriage until I am able to care for her."

"That is not my concern," Jacopo insisted. "If she loves you, she will wait."

Filippo thought his spirit had died with his father, but this betrayal truly killed it, for it killed his future with Sandrina. When her father, his own godfather, who had been so pleased by their union, learned that Filippo was a pauper, with barely enough money left to support his studies, he called off the engagement. In a week he betrothed Sandrina to a richer man in the village. The injustice of her inability to make her own choices in life never left Filippo's mind, and Sandrina never left his heart. Though other women would come and go from it, Sandrina and her smile stayed there for the rest of his life.

Dejected and alone, Filippo returned to school, and to a series of other girlfriends, each too similar to Sandrina to carve her own place in his life. Then, in an act designed to destroy him because he believed he deserved it, Filippo fell in love again—this time with Maria, a beautiful young woman he met at a party during Carnevale. But this was doomed from the start because Maria had a husband, nearly twice her age to be sure, but a husband in the eyes of the church all the same. The husband hired Filippo to give his young wife dancing lessons and Filippo was too weak to refuse. He grew to love Maria more and more during the clandestine kisses they shared during those dancing lessons, but soon dangerous rumors spread.

A man approached Filippo one night at a party as Filippo watched his lover use his dancing techniques in the arms of her husband across the room. This man whispered the rumor of Maria's infidelity, but when he named the illicit lover, it was another man. Filippo staunchly defended Maria's honor, but in his heart he realized the truth of the slander. Maria had begged off a series of recent lessons in order to study pottery. It devastated Filippo to hear she had used the same excuses he had heard her give her husband in order to see Filippo. Yet out of loyalty to Maria, Filippo demanded satisfaction for her honor as a stand-in for her husband.

At that time most men in Italy carried their swords with them, and that night was no different. Each man already had his weapon at the ready. So Filippo and the accuser stepped out into the darkened street to duel. Once away from the noise of the party, however, the man quickly apologized for his accusations and disappeared down the street.

Whether it was Sandrina's inability to choose her own husband or his brother's ability to control his life as head of the family or the mean way Maria had used him, Filippo began to form ideas about individual freedom and natural liberty. Were not all humans created equal in the eyes of God?

One instance that added to this ideology happened on one of his weekly trips to the Jewish quarter of Florence, to the shop of Salomon Balloffi, whose son, Beniamino, had become a great friend to Filippo.

As he approached the shop, Filippo called to his friend. "Beniamino! *Come stai?*"

But Beniamino did not respond. He was far too focused on throwing a punch at a ruffian who stood outside the store, slamming a stick into the cart full of fresh figs. Filippo hurried down the street.

"*Basta!*" shouted Beniamino.

Filippo could not make out the response as the ruffian faced away from him, but he could tell by the body language that it wasn't a compliment.

Salomon came to the door of the store and yelled for his son to let it go, to let the guild men police the situation, but

Beniamino wouldn't lower his fists. The ruffian slammed his stick into Beniamino's stomach, knocking him to the ground, stunned. When Salomon ran to his son, the ruffian moved to slam the stick into Salomon's balding head. Filippo caught the ruffian off guard, slamming the flat of his sword across the man's back. The attacker stumbled forward as Beniamino stood up shakily. Now faced with two young men as opponents and a growing crowd of onlookers, the ruffian turned and ran, tossing a final, angry epithet as he rounded the corner. Filippo moved to follow him, but Salomon held him back.

"Leave him to his hate," Salomon said. When Filippo hesitated, clearly wanting to chase the other man, Salomon urged him otherwise. "Help me get Beni into the house. And thank you."

Filippo tried to brush off the gratitude, but Salomon continued. "An act of grace is an act of grace. Let an old man show his appreciation."

"I did nothing out of the ordinary but show my loyalty to two good friends," Filippo insisted. "What kind of a world do we live in that a simple act of humanity and justice seems a surprising feat?"

"This world," Salomon said.

Filippo wasn't sure if that was a sad reflection or a challenge.

He didn't have time to ponder that question for long, however, because his own situation grew more challenging on his next trip home to see his mother and sister. He found them in greatly reduced circumstances. Jacopo, now in charge of their affairs, had fired the once-a-week help and had the ladies doing their own cooking and cleaning of the house each day, even as Mama grew older and took on that bent back so common in the peasant women of the village.

Instead of being angry with Jacopo, or even disappointed, Elisabetta loved him all the more for being the one at home. In her mind Jacopo was the one who sacrificed his position to come and care for them while Filippo had returned to his frivolous life in Florence.

"But Mama," Filippo said, trying not to raise his voice or be disrespectful, "I am nearly finished with my studies."

"Those so-called 'studies,' all those girlfriends, they have ruined us," she said. "And then to take your part of the inheritance early…what will happen when Vittoria needs to marry?"

Filippo realized he had heard the same sentiments from Jacopo during their father's funeral; now his mother was echoing them. "When I'm a surgeon I will send money," he countered. "I'm almost done. But even now, come and live with me. I will care for you. You will love Florence."

Filippo argued all morning to no avail, finally cutting it off in time to begin the bread-making for the peasants, a tradition he missed while in Florence. But Filippo learned that not only had Jacopo ended the family's benevolence, he had also padlocked the pantry to prevent their mother from giving even a slice of bread to any poor person who came knocking. This was the final blow. While Filippo had learned to be a benefactor from their grandfather, Jacopo's philosophy had become "whoever wanted to eat his bread had to earn it."

When Jacopo said this to Filippo with that tinge of arrogance only Filippo seemed to hear, Filippo wanted to beat his brother into the ground. Instead, seeing the futility in fighting when his mother's mind would never change, Filippo said quietly, "By saying that, you have killed Nonno again."

Then he turned to his mother sadly. "Goodbye, Mother. May God reward you as you deserve for your behavior toward me. If you will not listen to me, if you will not see the error of these choices, I will spend the rest of my life proving you have given all your love to the wrong son."

Chapter Three

ON HIS OWN, YET NEVER ALONE

Filippo returned to Florence, unsure where he belonged anymore. Thanks to the stories Jacopo had spread to his family and friends while he was away, Filippo felt he could no longer live among the people of Poggio. He realized the only way to fight Jacopo was with money and he needed to earn his own, but there were already too many practicing surgeons in Florence. And Filippo wasn't even sure he still wanted to be a surgeon. Making a living would be more difficult for both those reasons. To top it off, in his heart, Filippo loved the quiet of a small town, the beauty of fields that flowed on forever, the long conversations over dinner in a friend's garden. How far would he need to go to create such a life for himself?

He pondered the question over pasta with fellow medical students Gregori and Michelini and his friends Beniamino and David. The group often met at Caffè dello Svizzerino, near the Church of San Michele and down the street from Beniamino's family store in the Jewish quarter.

One night David did not appear. The café owner told them David's mother was gravely ill and the whole family had been called to her side. The group immediately headed to David's father's house to see if they could be of service. There were always things to do when someone was dying: prepare coffee for those sitting in wait, make meals, say the rosary. Though in this case Filippo remembered that David and his family, being Jewish, could do without the rosary. It was an early reminder that being free to worship as you chose was part of that freedom and natural liberty that kept cropping up in conversations.

Upon arriving at the house, Filippo found that his friendship wasn't needed as urgently as his medical studies were. While the local doctor, untrained outside of years of apprenticeship, had declared David's mother to be at death's door, Filippo read her breathing to mean she had broken the fever and was on her way back to health. David and his family hugged and thanked Filippo for making that discovery, and in the days to come, brought food to his rooms to thank him, along with more patients.

"But I didn't cure her," Filippo begged off the compliments. "I simply recognized—"

"I know that," David interrupted, dropping off a delicious torte made by his sister-in-law. "But you used your talents to relieve our stress when a supposedly more experienced man did not. You have a gift."

"But I'm still not sure if it's the gift I'm meant to pursue."

"Take it one day at a time. One patient at a time. A path will become clear. And you will know it is the one to follow."

As if David had foreseen it, a new opportunity came to Filippo that very week. While he was visiting Beniamino again in his father's shop, Beni's uncle Abramo arrived. Shortly after they all shared an espresso, Abramo collapsed. Beniamino ran for Dr. Cocchi, but he was not home. Instead, Dr. Scodillari came, the same doctor who had misread David's mother's symptoms.

Scodillari promptly diagnosed a need to bleed Abramo as a cure. Filippo disagreed vehemently.

Scodillari demanded his cure be followed under threat of losing Abramo. It was only Filippo's long-term friendship with Beniamino and Salomon that swayed the family to take his side. Scodillari left angrily and Filippo ran for Dr. Cocchi.

When Cocchi completed his treatment, he rose and faced Salomon, who thanked him profusely for saving his brother's life.

"It is my calling," said Cocchi. "But don't waste all your thanks on me. Young Mazzei here stopped the fool from making things worse." He looked over at Filippo. "That's twice you corrected Scodillari. We ought to give you a medal."

"I'd settle for…" Filippo wasn't sure how to end that sentence once he'd started it. Home? Family? A path? He already had friends—that much he could now see.

"A practice?" Cocchi completed the sentence. "I have a friend in Livorno, on the coast, who is too old to keep up the pace of a modern surgeon. I could write you a letter of introduction."

Livorno? The coast? Could he go that far? Filippo remembered all the days of sitting with his tutor, dreaming of going even farther, even to the American colonies. How better to begin a life's journey across the ocean than by living near one for a while? Filippo recalled a local Florentine who had traveled to South America and returned quite well-off financially. He also remembered that he had cousins living in Livorno whom he had rarely seen—and whom Jacopo had rarely seen, and therefore hadn't had the chance of poisoning them against him.

So Filippo packed his meager belongings and said goodbye to Salomon and Beniamino, to Raimondo—and to the memory of both Sandrina and Maria. He took a boat from Florence to

Pisa and a small stagecoach to Livorno. When Filippo stepped off the stagecoach, he turned to the driver. "I've never been farther than fifteen miles from my father's house. Everything is as new to me as China and Japan could be."

The driver smiled as he handed Filippo his trunk. "Then make the most of it, my young friend. Most people never live farther than the city of their birth, and most die there. From all the passengers I've carried, I've learned how big this world is. Why shouldn't one see as much of it as he can?"

Filippo smiled at the thought, and at the way the driver chuckled over his own words, as he took his first steps on what seemed like foreign land. It was good practice for other steps he would someday take in even farther lands. At least here he knew the language, though that would come to be less true the longer he resided in Livorno.

He also knew his cousins, Domenico and Vincenzo, sons of his uncle Pietro, who turned out to be far kinder to him than he ever could have hoped. Domenico had made his name as a chocolatier. Having spent time in the navy and traveled, he brought back some of the secrets of the chocolatiers of Modica, a small town in the southeastern part of the Kingdom of Sicily. There the locals made chocolate with recipes and techniques brought back by a Spanish conquistador who settled in Modica when the land was under Spanish rule. He made chocolates the way the Aztecs of Tenochtitlan did, by using smooth round stones to grind cacao into a paste called *xocoàtl*. Domenico added more bitter spices to his chocolate so it could accompany meats as an exotic sauce. He also sold dessert chocolates, and eventually, in partnership with Vincenzo, expanded the store into an apothecary, so their shop enjoyed frequent return customers.

Domenico and Vincenzo befriended Filippo and introduced him to former friends and business associates of his father, including the foremost English merchant in the city. He met both the local abbot, a good friend of his brother Giuseppe who had now fully entered the priesthood, and the Marquis de Silva of the Spanish Consulate. As to his profession, he came under the wing of the popular and successful Dr. Cei. All eagerly helped the young man begin his surgical practice as he settled into the historic city, named by the Romans for one of their naval ships, which, in turn, had been named for the ancient Illyrian tribe that once inhabited the area. The Illyrian kingdom, led by King Agron, used the boats to attack Greek and Roman interests in the Adriatic Sea. The Romans, impressed by the swift galleys they first fought with when they entered the Adriatic, adopted this style of ship during the Punic Wars and it gave them further mastery of the seas.

For those uninterested in all things military, Livorno offered many other experiences, and Filippo intended to make the most of them. He chose a home in Venezia Nuova, in a one-hundred-year-old district, because of his fascination with the canals and bridges linking all parts of the town. It had taken Venetian workers many years to create such a system back in the early 1600s. The district also housed the Consuls of the Nations, where retailers stored their goods before transport. Filippo enjoyed watching the unloading of products from distant lands onto his shores, often wondering about the people and places from which the products originated. As the major port city on the coast, Livorno boasted visitors from all over the world. The British had reestablished trade in the last fifty years, though they called the town Leghorn. In order to work and socialize with the British philosophers and writers who formed the expatriate community, Filippo learned English and discovered he had a facility with language, which would prove valuable later in life.

Surrounded by this cosmopolitan world, Filippo soon found his interest in medicine as a vocation fading, but as that was the reputation he brought with him to Livorno, it was how he continued to make his living. Dr. Cei offered to refer patients to Filippo the day they met, when the doctor came to Vincenzo's apothecary for some medicinal herbs.

"But why would you send patients—and therefore profits— away to another doctor?" asked Domenico, who had the better head for business.

"A surgeon can be very busy in Livorno, it's true," Cei explained. "And he can make much money, as several do. But he does his patients a disservice if he takes them on knowing he does not have the time or attention to do the job well."

Filippo took that lesson to heart in all his future dealings. The quality he most respected in his mentor surgeon—natural enthusiasm for people and for life—became one Filippo tried the most to emulate.

He had an opportunity to practice that enthusiasm with his first patient in Livorno, a nine-year-old boy named Serafino, from a poor family who lived around the corner from his cousin's store. The child had broken his humerus, the bone between the elbow and the shoulder that Filippo thought the easiest to set inside the entire human body. It was even the easiest to bandage tightly and neatly.

While Filippo wrapped the bandage around the boy's arm with a bit of flair, he diagnosed the real problem in his mind: poverty. The family clearly did not have sufficient money to provide enough meat for the boy—and his bones—to grow strong. But how could he make this point without harming the mother's pride?

"Signora Barola," said Filippo, "the bandage will hold the bone in place as it heals."

"*Grazie, grazie!*" Signora Barola exclaimed, and went on repeating herself for a while. "*Grazie, grazie.*"

"You are welcome," Filippo interrupted gently, "but he will need more than that. He will need good beef broth for a few weeks to strengthen the bone." Filippo saw the light in her eyes fade and knew she could not afford the meat to make broth so often. He quickly continued, "My cousin, Domenico, often has extra beef from testing his new chocolate sauce recipes, but cannot then sell it for want of a butcher's license. You would do him a favor if you returned every Tuesday and took away his excess. Would that be agreeable?"

Signora Barola smiled and quickly agreed.

As expected, the bone mended perfectly and the mother became a walking advertisement for Filippo's services, telling everyone she saw how this new young surgeon had come to Livorno by the grace of God.

So Filippo filled his days with patients referred to him by Dr. Cei, or by his cousins or by Signora Barola, and filled his nights with conversations over coffee or with reading all he could about philosophy and history—and medicine. He had secretly decided that practicing medicine was not for him, yet it was the way he currently made his living and so he worked to be good at it for the sake of his patients. His latest find had been published that year, 1752, by an Italian living in France, so Filippo slowly taught himself to read French in order to read Natale Giuseppe Pallucci's *Method of Extracting Cataracts*. He loved the feel of the gold-tooled leather binding as the book rested in his palm. It made reading both an artistic and an educational pursuit.

At his cousin's apothecary and during dinners with new-found friends from all over the world, Filippo learned much about the workings of government and how it handled religion differently in various places. He found himself more and more fascinated by the idea that so many different ideas took precedence all over the world, even to the point of deciding what day it was. The big news that year came when Britain finally agreed to use the Gregorian calendar that most of the continent had adopted when Pope Gregory XIII required all of Catholic Europe to do so with his papal bull of 1582. Not being a Catholic country, Britain had clung to the Julian calendar, but found it difficult to do business being fourteen days off from nearly everyone else's calculations.

"A government must be led by one religion," Vincenzo said one day, "or the people will fall away from the church."

"Which church are they falling from?" Filippo questioned. "Even in this city we do business daily with people of different faiths…Jews, Muslims…I've even had a Buddhist patient. Remember, he had fallen ill and no one knew his religion, so they brought him to me. How can one government tell all of them how to live their own lives in their own homes?"

"Bravo, Filippo," said one of his new friends, Dr. Salinas. "As a man of the Jewish faith, I try to be open to the thoughts of the other sons of Abraham—wrong-headed though they may be." The oldest of the group at sixty-four, Salinas often teased his young friends.

"Which of us is wrong-headed?" asked the smiling Marquis de Silva, the Spanish consulate who came to their weekly debate dinners for the quality of both the debate and the wine

Domenico collected. "That is far too honest an opinion to give in public, my friend of another faith. When asked questions of a controversial nature, my philosophy is to give my answer in such a way as not to injure the self-esteem of anyone else at my table."

"I see nothing injurious in saying religion is a private matter," Filippo said.

"That's an opinion best kept to oneself in places like England," Silva replied. "You do know how many Catholics King Henry VII executed, don't you?"

"What about the many Protestants they executed when Bloody Mary came into power?" asked Salinas.

"Luckily, neither monarch did anything to the Jews of England," Domenico said. "They are everywhere there today." As he was not as interested in world affairs as his peers, and not as well read, Domenico was often contradicted in these debates, but he always took it well.

This time Filippo did the contradicting. "Cousin, Henry and his daughter did nothing to the Jews because they had all been expelled from the country by King Edward nearly two centuries earlier. Those we know today were only allowed back by Cromwell over a hundred years ago."

Salinas added, "Well, not all of us left the island. I have Spanish cousins in my family history who remained Jewish in private, but pretended Christianity in public."

"Exactly," seconded Silva. "There are still Spanish families who think themselves Jewish, but I believe if you followed their lineage back far enough, you would find the original Catholics."

"Why should anyone be forced to hide who they are?" Filippo posed the question. "Why should any monarch require their citizens to deny such a personal choice? We have Jews in most of the duchies, yet we live much closer to the Pope than any other nation."

"That's a question to be solved by far smarter men than we are," said Salinas, not often one to be so modest. "Today I have an easier question to pose to our friend Filippo."

"Why me?" Filippo asked.

"You are the only other medical man at this table," Salinas answered. "You please your patients, which brings profits both financial and fulfilling. I am returning to Turkey in the next months and I need such a man in my practice there."

"*Complimenti*," Vincenzo and Domenic saluted Filippo together.

"Who knew we had such a cousin?" Vincenzo added.

"I thank you for your compliment, but I've not been at Livorno for long," Filippo began.

"You say you want to see the world, see how government works in other places. When do you plan to start?" Salinas asked.

Silva added, "Travel enriches the soul…and can only be done when one has no family to leave behind, no wife, no children, free—as you are today, Filippo."

"But, truth be told, I am fascinated with the English colonies in the Americas," Filippo admitted. "Of late, my thoughts have been to witness this for myself."

Vincenzo, the better-read of the two brothers, interjected. "Ha! The Americas. We in Livorno don't forget the folly of Ferdinand the First. A colony in South America. Ridiculous. A failure. The grandchildren of the men who followed that folly still live in disgrace in the city one hundred and fifty years after that failure."

Silva added, "My friend, you are far too straightforward and have yet to have the experience to go to Spain or Portugal, much less to these primitive colonies. What wine will you drink? What food will you eat in such a wasteland? Test yourself in Turkey, under the guidance of a learned man such as our friend here."

In the end Filippo took the advice of his small circle of counselors and agreed to undertake the journey to Smyrna on the central west coast of Turkey on the Aegean Sea, with Dr. Salinas financing two-thirds of the cost of the travel by land and taking two-thirds of the profit once in practice. Filippo was still uncommitted to medicine as his life's work, but for now it kept providing well, so he stayed dedicated to doing his best—and wondered where else it would lead him.

Chapter Four

TRAVELS IN TURKEY

In August 1752, Filippo set out with Dr. Salinas for the city of Smyrna at the northeastern corner of the inner Gulf of İzmir, at the edge of a fertile plain that had encouraged human habitation in the area since the eleventh century BC. Smyrna proper, still considered the new city by residents, had been founded on the inspiration of Alexander the Great in the fourth century BC.

To reach their new city, the two medical men passed through Bologna and Venice, then Vienna and Budapest before arriving in Constantinople, Turkey. While in Venice, Filippo and his companions toured the city and Filippo made a special point of acquiring a copy of Giambattista Marino's epic poem, *Adonis,* which he had heard was a very fine blending of new science and ancient romantic poetry. It took some work as none of his friends owned a copy, so Filippo haunted all the booksellers in the city until he found one he could own. But then their travels had to continue, so Filippo had to wait until their arrival in Smyrna to finally read the work, as the rocking motion in their wagon made reading impossible.

Traveling in winter created many an adventure and involved several hardships for the young man. The deep snow they encountered as they traveled through Austria became a concern. Inside one unexpectedly deep snowpack, the horses pulling the wagon full of Filippo's possessions—and Filippo—reared and the group spent a long afternoon repacking the wagon. The wet snow damaged some of their dry goods, leaving them low on provisions, and the experience brought Filippo a deep fatigue and eventually a fever. The group had to decamp to the home of a baron where Filippo could rest under the care of his mentor, Dr. Salinas.

Baron d'Aghilar, a Jewish man who served as treasurer to Maria Theresa, the Hapsburg queen of Austria, welcomed them warmly. While lying in his sick bed, Filippo and the baron talked medicine, religion, and politics. Filippo had never lived under a female ruler and hoped to observe the differences during his short stay. He found it interesting enough that the queen's father had had the foresight to create an edict as early as 1713 that ensured the Habsburg hereditary possessions could be inherited by a daughter. He wondered how long it would take other monarchies to rule the same.

"Never," the baron answered immediately. "At least not in England. The English queens have been accidents and no ruler will ever allow them to be next in line to succession since they are so frail and weak."

"But Queen Mary proved strong, though deadly to Catholics," said Filippo in a soft, tired voice.

"And to the Jews who were left around," the baron added. "Sleep now, my friend, and heal. We can talk of this another day."

Two weeks found Filippo ready to travel again and anxious to be back on the road.

"What's your hurry, my young friend?" Salinas asked the first day Filippo sat up in bed, talking of setting out again. "Having survived fever yet again, are you feeling immortal?"

"I'm just feeling…" Filippo searched for the right word, "…like I've been waiting to start my life, and somehow I keep waiting."

Salinas laughed heartily as he translated Filippo's comment into Turkish for the baron, who had been sitting beside the bed, checking up on his guest. Their caravan moved on quickly, so those ruminations would have to wait for another day and another visit.

On a happy note, they encountered some Italian regiments in Temesvar, Hungary, and Filippo relished the sound of his own language since he did not speak Turkish. Yet his feelings of dread were heightened as he approached the city, since it had been the site of the Christian massacre of 1552 while under Ottoman rule. Prince Eugene of Savoy conquered the area in 1716. By the time Filippo entered the territory in 1752, Temesvar belonged to Queen Maria Theresa, and times were much more stable. Being Italian, Filippo relished the local breads, which were almost as good as the ones they had baked fresh for the peasants back in Poggio.

Upon finally arriving in Turkey proper, Filippo found himself at the heart of the ancient yet still powerful Ottoman Empire, once again meeting a man of high importance. The fifty-six-year-old Sultan Mahmud I had been sultan since 1730 and had already befriended Salinas on a previous trip. Mahmud's father was Mustafa II; his mother was Saliha Sabkati, the Valide Sultan (the title held by the "legal mother" of a ruling sultan of the Ottoman Empire). The title was first used in the sixteenth century for Hafsa Sultan, consort of Selim I and mother of

Suleiman the Magnificent. Mahmud invited the caravan to enter the court of Edirne Palace as they settled into life in the region, on the west bank of the Tunca river. Though building had begun in 1450 during the reign of Murad II, each successive ruler had added new structures, such that Filippo counted seventy-two buildings, one hundred and seventeen rooms, fourteen mansions, eighteen bathhouses, eight mosques, seventeen gates, and thirteen cellars. Mahmud told him that at last count some 34,000 people lived in and around the palace with around 6,000 servants to care for them, more or less.

As he would across his lifetime, Filippo moved easily among the well-to-do and became the darling of court. Life at the palace intrigued Filippo as it seemed exotic yet normal to him, having read much about the Medici dukes of his own home country who ruled before the takeover of Francis of Lorraine in 1737.

Whenever Filippo visited Mahmud in the palace, he found the sultan deep in the work of writing poetry. "Each word must be the perfect word to follow the word that came before it or the job is not done," Mahmud said.

Filippo often counseled his new friend. Together they read Marino's *Adonis* and marveled at the mastery with which the artist had incorporated elements of Dante's *Inferno,* a poem Filippo knew well from his many years of private study.

"But why poetry?" Filippo asked the sultan one day as they worked on translating more of the *Adonis* into Turkish.

"Having come to power in a rage of violence and rebellion, which included watching the strangling of the general who brought me to power," the sultan began in a quiet, thoughtful, yet slightly sarcastic voice, "I prefer to leave the military work to my viziers."

"I understand that desire," Filippo answered. "I just meant why poetry and not painting?"

"He knows I like the art of words," said Rami Kadin, the youngest and boldest of Mahmud's six consorts, who all sat nearby as the men conversed.

Filippo found himself most fond of Rami, who enjoyed poetry but also found medicine as fascinating as Filippo did. Naturally, they only conversed in the presence of the sultan, who seemed happy to show off his elegant, intelligent young wife to his Italian friend. The sultan did not seem to mind when they discussed religion, for Filippo found it fascinating that, while Mahmud was a Muslim, almost all the consorts purchased for him in the slave markets were Christians.

Sadly, it was soon time to leave Mahmud and his court behind and move on to Smyrna, by way of Constantinople. There Filippo and Salinas met and befriended the Mullah of Constantinople, religious leader of the largest mosque in the area. Being the curious soul he was, Filippo would have enjoyed spending more time here, but Salinas, mindful of the weather, urged them forward.

"Why worry over weather when we can do nothing to change it?" Filippo asked.

"It is also true," Salinas replied, "that until we arrive in Smyrna we are spending more of my money while not making much to replenish the stores."

So despite his desire to learn as much about all the new cultures they encountered, Filippo agreed they should move on. The Mullah sent them off after a large feast, and provided the surgeons with letters of introduction to use in Smyrna to establish their credentials. Filippo's last impression of the city came from aboard deck as they set off on the Sea of Marmara.

It was faster in this area to travel by barge into the Aegean Sea since Smyrna sat on the coast. On the night he left the city, a huge fire erupted in the area of town where the merchants of oils, fats, tar, and turpentine resided. Filippo watched the flames from aboard deck.

Turning his mind toward the future, Filippo was happy when the barge approached the port of Smyrna after several rocky days at sea. Filippo had read all he could about the place he had promised the next few years of his life. While the city had belonged to the Aeolians and later the Ionians in ancient times, his interest centered on the time of Alexander the Great, around fourth century BC. That a place could have been designed so long ago, and settled fully for so long, amazed him. He wondered about those ancient tribes of Greece and how they had lived and loved. As he stood on the deck, Filippo also wondered how and whether he would thrive here, but his friendship with Dr. Salinas and the Mullah's letters of introduction seemed destined to make that happen.

"Smyrna of the infidels, eh, my young friend," said Salinas as he arrived on deck to watch their docking procedure.

"If Muslims and Christians can live together in the court of Mahmud," said Filippo, "I imagine they can live together in one city."

"True," said Salinas. "And it will be our job to help them in all ways we can. Men of medicine have a commitment to their patients to assist them in all facets of life."

That was only one of many lessons Filippo would learn in his life in Smyrna. The obligation of those in power to help those without power had weighed heavily on him since watching the difference in the ways his beloved grandfather and his detested brother Jacopo handled the peasants in his hometown. In Smyrna, the lesson solidified.

One day Filippo went to the local Greek grocer for a bit of lamb for his lunch and found a crowd gathered in the street around the store. As he approached, he heard the muttering. "That's what he gets for short-weighting our meat," several bystanders seemed to be saying.

"What has happened?" Filippo asked one of them.

"Didn't you hear?" the man demanded. "Sergei has been hung."

As the man spoke, Filippo saw the truth of what he said for himself. He gazed inside the shop and saw the grocer's legs dangling above the counter that held the scale.

"But this seems far afield to the penalty for one such occurrence," argued Filippo.

"Ah, but it was not only once," answered the man. "Sergei short-weighted Agostino's beef last week."

"Could people not simply have stopped patronizing his store?" mused Filippo aloud.

"He might learn from that, but who else would?" replied the man.

A few weeks later, a similar event drove home the discussion of justice. The town vizier ordered a baker accused of baking light loaves to bake all his bread in the vizier's personal oven, often in his presence, from then on.

"Are you then sure that they will not do it again?" Filippo asked the vizier, a frequent guest at Salinas's dinner table.

"No, we are not sure," said the vizier, "but we double the fine for a second offense and sometimes we even imprison the culprit.

I assure you that for at least ten years every baker in Constantinople will be afraid to make a short-weight loaf of bread."

While Filippo fulfilled his contract with Dr. Salinas by seeing and treating all the patients sent to him, he also took time to study the city. On quiet days, Filippo found he enjoyed walking in the local mountains that surrounded the town on three sides, leaving only the opening to the sea on which he had arrived. From his vantage point near the peak on Pagus, Filippo looked down upon the city and thought it looked as if it had sprung up all of a sudden into being, so full and uniform in all its parts. The sea seemed to creep up yearningly, seeking to engulf the city in its warm embrace. He thought often of the poetry Mahmud could make of this sight and that reminded him of how meeting new people was as much the delight of travel as the opportunity to bask in such exotic scenery.

That pull to travel tugged at Filippo more and more, so that after two years in Turkey, he told Salinas, "I want to see other lands and peoples."

His mentor smiled sadly. "It is not as if I didn't expect that to happen. Perhaps if we renew our contract and I offer more advantageous terms…."

Filippo, too, smiled sadly, but said no.

"I will deeply miss our association," said a resigned Salinas. "But it is true that our contracted time is at an end and you have done all you promised to aide my patients and enhance my standing in the community. Where will you go?"

"Remember when the marquis told me I was not yet seasoned enough for the colonies?" Filippo asked. When Salinas nodded, the young man continued. "I believe I have done as he asked, tested myself in Turkey, and survived."

"But our dear friend said after Turkey you'd be ready for his country, or Portugal," Salinas reminded him.

"Or the colonies," Filippo reminded back. "Being Italian I have read the history of the duchies of Italy, I have read the rise of Spain—and Portugal. They are old and honorable civilizations. But in the colonies, there are rumblings of the beginnings of yet another civilization. Can you imagine being at the start of such a moment in history?"

"Your eyes tell the story," said Salinas. "You are ready to make your mark on the world and I understand that requires new lands and new people. Go with my blessing."

Retracing his steps from Smyrna through Turkey, Filippo stopped at the Topkapi Palace in Constantinople, where his last letter from Mahmud I had originated. He intended to make his farewells, only to find his old friend on his deathbed at the young age of fifty-eight. He watched the peaceful passing of power, something he would be pleased to witness again through governmental law rather than death when he met and befriended many of the early presidents of the United States. Though his new journey would begin in England, it would culminate in Filippo's deep love, devotion, and dedication to pursuing freedom for those colonists in North America.

Chapter Five

A NEW LIFE IN LONDON

In order to conserve funds, Filippo decided to travel to England by serving as a ship's doctor. He signed on with Captain Wilson for five guineas a month and a space in the hold for products from Livorno that Filippo could sell in London for profit. Unbeknownst to him, it was the beginning of his future business as a merchant.

Before departure, rumors of impending war between England and France ran rampant, so Wilson applied for and received a pirate's permit, allowing him to equip the ship with twenty-two guns mounted on the sides for defense. This change in definition of the mission of the ship caused Filippo to reconsider this venue for travel. As did the fact that, though he would serve as the ship's surgeon, he was not comfortable with amputation, a frequent treatment for sailors' wounds. Wilson was not deterred.

"We are not likely to meet any warships as the hostilities have not yet reached that point, Mazzei," said the captain in Spanish, for he spoke no Italian and Filippo as yet spoke no English. "I have heard many good things about you, and the letters of recommendation you have collected to begin your life in London are of the highest caliber. Trust me as I trust you and it will be a fine voyage."

Filippo responded in Portuguese, one of the other languages they both shared. "I thank you for those well-chosen words and look forward to the trip."

In his space on the ship, Filippo stored products he heard would sell well in London, including red raisins, dried figs, and opium. Near the end of December, they set sail along with two Irish vessels that needed the protection of the guns. They spent three days in Argentiera, a town on the coast of Sardinia, to repair one of the Irish ships and to attend Mass. There Filippo found one of his unexpected duties as surgeon.

When Captain Wilson, not being Catholic, chose not to attend Mass, but rather to sample the wares of one of the bordellos on the island, Filippo took him aside and whispered, "I feel it is my duty to warn you of the risk to your health that such an assignation will create."

Captain Wilson laughed a deep-throated laugh and responded as one more seasoned than Filippo. "I do not wish to reproach myself later with the thought that I had visited such an exotic place and not learned what the local ladies are like." He winked at Filippo as he walked away, but Filippo knew he personally would not be involved in such exchanges during this—or any—voyage.

A hard storm met them as they passed Malta, and Filippo was forced to stay locked in his cabin as the captain spent the frightful night tacking the boat back and forth to avoid capsizing. They survived that night only to face a furious wind in the Bay of Biscay that rendered their rudder useless. Two young apprentice sailors, ages ten and eight, were ordered to climb the sails and furl the foresails, securing them as neatly as possible to survive the wind. The younger of the two could barely hold his own as he climbed against the wind and was thrown back twice, landing in the folds of the sail high above Filippo's head. On his way down he did fall to the deck, but from a close enough height that the boy remained conscious.

As Filippo checked him for broken bones, he asked the eight-year-old in French, as neither spoke English, "Why, when you saw the winds were against you, did you not climb down out of danger immediately?"

The young boy repeated what he had been taught. "One must never come down until the captain's orders have been carried out."

Captain Wilson chuckled upon hearing this and gave the boy, who proved to have no broken bones, an extra guinea for his efforts.

When the boy left his quarters, Filippo smiled at the captain. "I no longer wonder at England's superiority at sea. Clearly, I chose the right passage—and the right captain."

Filippo and the captain weathered one more storm as they entered the English Channel, and Filippo learned that English seamen considered this strip of water the most dangerous of all they encountered. The storm finally subsided, and Captain Wilson landed the ship in the London docks on March 2, 1756. Instead of things going smoothly now that they had arrived, another incident required Filippo's ability to negotiate rather than use his surgical skills. Upon arrival, the crew of Wilson's boat were impressed into the British Navy, a legal act before the outbreak of and during a war. Among the crew Filippo knew of four Italian sailors whom he felt should not be forced to serve a country not their own. He asked Captain Wilson for the chance to negotiate for the men.

"I doubt it will do any good," said Wilson, "but you are a free man, as my crew is supposed to be, and if you can do anything to help your countrymen, it's not my place to stop you."

In one of the first of many providential moments of Filippo's life, he happened to have a letter of introduction from the Swedish Consul in Smyrna to a London merchant named John Chamier, who had spent several years' residency in Livorno. Being favorable to Italians, Chamier agreed to accompany Filippo to the Minister of the Marine, the officer in charge of the newly impressed sailors. There Filippo used his natural talent for talking to negotiate freedom for the four Italian soldiers and one from Malta whom he pretended was Italian.

Impressed with Filippo's success, Chamier invited him to a *conversazione* with one of the most learned men in London, Dr. Sharp, who at eighty knew more about world literature than any other man in attendance. Among the guests was Dr. May, a curator at the British Museum and an eminent anatomist. That evening the debate centered around something Filippo knew intimately—Dante's *Inferno*—which gave the newcomer a chance to showcase his own intellect against such a renowned gathering. Another young man in the group tried to argue that Dante was unintelligible and used a phrase quite trite in town to describe Italian poets as compared to those in England: "They are four hundred years behind the times."

Sharp did not take this insult to one of his literary heroes lightly, snapping back quickly, "When an author's merits are so many and so great, I should be ashamed to recall only his defects."

The room fell silent, with no man sure how to move the conversation in a new direction. To smooth the path, as was his way, Filippo offered the idea, "Perhaps the gentleman has read inferior translations or commentaries on Dante and has therefore come to this mistaken conclusion. I would be glad to suggest the commentary I read when I was a student at Pisa."

The other young man smiled at the opening Filippo gave him, promised to read the version suggested, and the whole group moved on to a dissection of the way Milton used Dante in his own works.

On their way home that evening, Chamier took Filippo aside.

"Your behavior impressed a good deal of useful men tonight," Chamier said. "On top of your success with the Minister of the Marine, I believe you have made quite a solid start to your time in London."

Returning to his small room at Captain Wilson's house that night, Filippo truly felt that London would do well for him. At home Jacopo always took the stage as the family scholar, relegating Filippo to the inferior position through his condescending tone of voice. Filippo knew that was what made people listen to his older brother, that ability to cut them down publicly if they did not listen, and he knew he'd have to manage that experience differently when he returned in order to convince his mother to trust him more with her affairs. Meanwhile, he would work on making enough money to take care of her so that Jacopo's continued guardianship would not be necessary.

To that end, in the daytime Filippo worked on selling the products he had transported from Tuscany, and with the help of Chamier, he made more money than he had hoped. At night, he worked on learning the English language through a method he invented. He would take a book written in English on a subject he knew well, usually medicine or literature, and copy out one whole chapter over and over. On the first copy he could recognize twenty or so words, but on the next he began to see by context what twenty more words meant, and on and on until he had copied the same chapter multiple times, until he understood all the words and, perhaps more importantly, as much of the grammar as possible. It was a system he would use throughout his life to learn other languages as his travels continued.

The other thing travel taught him was how hard it is for man to live by the philosophy he flaunts in conversation. England considered itself the land of public liberty where law always prevailed. While the English spouted that line over and over, when Filippo attended trials at Parliament he found the outcome often fell against the weaker defendant no matter what the law, or the judge in private, might claim. Filippo's first experience with disillusion came from the impressment of those Italian soldiers, who, thanks to his efforts, had been allowed to sail back to Italy on another crew. He was sure they would never again sign on to a boat headed to England, or France, as long as rumors of war rumbled across the sea.

"They claim we are four hundred years behind the times, but in Florence, such things do not happen," Filippo said to a new friend, Dr. Hunter, during dinner one night.

"Impressment is a matter of the public good," Hunter said, "so the public's benefit must always be the victor. Personal liberty is quite another matter, and the British Empire respects that more perfectly."

Because Filippo took the time to read widely on the debates in Parliament and also attend some trials in person, he found Hunter was correct: Personal liberty did seem to be honored. One such trial involved Lord Ferrers, a peer of the realm who shot and killed an agent on his estate. In Italy, such a crime would be mildly punished by restricting the royal to his own lands for a period of time. In England, the taking of another's life earned Ferrers the gallows. The idea that the life of a commoner was legally equal to the life of a lord pleased Filippo. He decided to relocate more permanently to London, renting a house on the edge of Westminster, and writing his relatives in Livorno to ship him more goods similar to those he brought with him on Captain Wilson's ship so that he could go into business as a merchant.

While he waited between shipments, Filippo took the advice of several of his new friends and began earning money teaching the Tuscan tongue to Londoners. At first he hesitated at the suggestion that he ought to teach for money. That idea was looked down upon in Tuscany.

But Dr. May insisted, "In England, a lazy person is not respected. Every honest occupation is held in high esteem and those most eminent in their fields are honored and ought to be paid what they are worth."

To May, lessons in Italian were worth anywhere between one and three guineas per twelve lessons. The older man also suggested that Filippo could make many new connections for his mercantile business by meeting people through the venue of teaching the language. So Filippo agreed and found he learned as much about English through teaching Italian as his clients learned about Italian.

True to May's word, through teaching Filippo met a banker who loaned him five hundred pounds to stabilize his business. When Filippo offered the man his promissory note for the loan, the banker threw the paper into the fireplace.

Filippo protested, "Life and death are not in our hands. Your family must be able to collect on my debts should you die."

"Do you think that if such misfortune should befall me that I could be bothered with such trifles?" joked the banker.

~

Just as Filippo's business in England was beginning to thrive and his acquaintances filled his lunches and dinners with engaging conversation, he had to quit the city to return home, thanks to a letter from his sister, Vittoria. It seemed their mother and her finances suffered under Jacopo's control. In her own words, Vittoria begged Filippo to "return and deliver our mother from the hands of her favorite and unworthy son."

Filippo headed back to Italy immediately, passing through the Austrian and French Flanders and Paris before boarding a boat in Marseilles, France, bound for Livorno. Once again, a storm interrupted his travel plans and the boat went aground in Genoa, Italy. From there Filippo traveled by stagecoach to Florence, where Vittoria, her husband, and their three-year-old child resided on Via dell'Oriuolo. Before he could ask directions to the exact house, Filippo glimpsed his uncle, Father Mazzei, watching out the window for his arrival.

At the door the two men embraced and his uncle exclaimed, "My nephew, I have ruined you."

It seemed his uncle had legally handed his own inheritance from Filippo's father inter vivos, or as a gift of the living, to Jacopo in order to help finance the needs of Filippo's mother. Now he regretted leaving her care in Jacopo's hands and the feeling brought him to tears in Filippo's presence.

"Do not weep, dear uncle," Filippo comforted him. "Rather rejoice with me that I have need of nothing. I am happier in the possession of what little I have—because I have earned it all myself—than I could be with the whole of the estates of my father."

With his sister, Filippo was equally comforting. He enjoyed meeting his brother-in-law, Mario Saladini, for the first time at dinner that night. Mario had studied pharmacy at the university and now worked in Filippo's old stomping ground, the Santa Maria Nuova Hospital, so they enjoyed a long conversation over after-dinner hot chocolate. As Vittoria poured the thick chocolate into the tiny white cups, Filippo and Mario discussed Nuova and some of the people they jointly knew. Filippo found Mario honest and kind in both word and deed, especially in the act of marrying Vittoria though Jacopo had defrauded her of the dowry promised to her in their father's will. Filippo cut the visit short in order to travel to Jacopo's house to see their mother.

Jacopo met him at the door, his usual conniving nature preceding him. "Brother, why did you not come to your home at once?"

Deeply insulted by the hypocrisy of Jacopo referring to the home he stole from him as "your home," Filippo wanted to give him a good blow on the chin, but decided against doing that in earshot of their fragile mother. Instead, he avoided Jacopo's embrace and entered the home to find his mother sitting quietly by the fire. His eyes understood in an instant the shabbiness of her clothing and the fear in her eyes as Jacopo entered behind him.

"Mother, just look at our Filippo," Jacopo began in that sugary-sweet voice that Filippo had learned to detest. "At last we have the joy of seeing him again. Isn't it true, mother?"

"Yes, sir," Elisabetta said in a monotone, more muscle memory than true conversational contribution.

Jacopo began monopolizing the conversation, describing all the wondrous things he had been doing for their mother, things that required sacrificing his own career. Filippo tried several times to steer the conversation back to his mother and her care, but each time Jacopo answered for their mother and added, "Isn't that right, mother?" she responded, "Yes, sir." When Filippo could take it no more, he announced that Vittoria had asked him to bring their mother back to her home for a short visit with her grandchild and Filippo could escort her the next morning as he had a business appointment there the next day.

"How well timed," replied Jacopo. "Mother will require a couple of days to prepare for such a journey and I am traveling to Florence in two days' time. You can return tomorrow and I will escort Mother on Friday."

Filippo angered himself at being caught in another of Jacopo's cons. He shouldn't have said he had to leave. Now Jacopo had an out for letting their mother accompany him so soon. All Filippo could do was take his leave of them, return to Florence, and await their arrival.

In Prato, en route to Florence, Filippo became melancholy at the sound of the bells that used to ring at his school each day. He had always been quite sad at school. The mood suited his feelings about his family situation.

In Florence, Filippo bided his time meeting new business partners who were impressed with the English products he had sent back to Italy and wanted to create stronger commerce between the two areas. Tuscan wines and olive oils had become sought after in London and Filippo's cousins in Livorno could handle the exportation of enough for a financially viable deal. He filled his days with the legalities of such contracts and his nights with reading a new drama from his old friend Abbot Coltelini. By the end of Filippo's stay in the city, Coltelini had taken most of his suggestions about tightening the manuscript.

Coltelini thanked him with a smile. "Do not think that there are not men here capable of this task, but where else was I to find another person who can fling the truth in one's face as you can?"

It was the beginning of Filippo's interest in writing and his understanding that he had a particular felicity for the art.

Yet in the end, it all felt like an empty exercise as he waited and waited for a mother who never came. Filippo sent letters when she didn't arrive and his mother sent back excuses involving business and her health in an endless cycle of exchanges. Filippo knew Jacopo dictated the letters and feared he forced their mother to write them, but not being her legal guardian, Filippo had no legal right to challenge his brother. Filippo even succeeded in having his brother Giuseppe, the Capuchin monk, take a leave from the monastery to visit him and their mother in the city.

Three months of haggling over her visit ended when Elisabetta finally arrived in Florence. Sadly, Filippo and Giuseppe soon realized Jacopo had kept her home long enough to brainwash her into believing he was the only one who could truly care for her. She admitted to her other sons that her treatment up to that time had not been kind, but assured them that this visit had enlightened Jacopo and she had accepted his promise to change.

"Dear mother, be merciful to yourself," Giuseppe told her. "Do not make this dreadful mistake. You will only be treated worse than you were before as soon as we are gone and there will be no one to defend you. In my position, having taken a vow of poverty, I can do nothing for you. Filippo has come all the way from England expressly for you, and the journey from London to Florence is no pleasure trip. Trust him who has shown you his true self."

Even this did not persuade Elisabetta and so Filippo had to take his leave.

"Unfortunately, what my dear brother has prophesied will come to pass," Filippo said. "That monster of a brother has been masquerading to the public for so long, he will have to take it out on someone when we are gone, and that someone will be you, dear mother. I can only ask that no one informs me further of his behavior for I could not but be grieved, and I do not deserve that after all I have done in vain for you."

And with that, he kissed his mother goodbye and he was gone.

Chapter Six

ITALY AND THE INQUISITION

Dejected and disillusioned about his family, Filippo returned to London, and in 1764 he opened a shop selling imported Italian wares including wine and olive oil. He named the shop Martini & Company to avoid incurring a reputation as merely a shopkeeper, since he still didn't know what the future would hold. While he had decided not to pursue medicine anymore, he felt he had simply fallen into business and wanted to stay open to other opportunities as they arose.

Being bereft of a family of his own, Filippo found himself eager to make a family of the friends he gathered around him in his travels and here in his new home in London. The first benefactors of this desire were the Martin family. The father was hired on to paint and wallpaper Filippo's new home in London, and then he rented the upstairs for himself, his wife, and two daughters. Sadly, the younger daughter died before she reached her first birthday and the painter became so distraught that he, too, took to his deathbed six months later. There he bemoaned the fact that he had nothing to leave his widow and daughter besides the furniture in their rooms. Kneeling at the bedside, Filippo said, "I will never abandon your family as long as I am in a position to help." The promise seemed to ease the man's pain and he died later that night.

True to his word, Filippo allowed the widow, Mrs. Martin, and her daughter, Maria Margherita, to continue to live in the rooms for free, and Filippo also paid for Maria's education so that she could make a successful match someday. Mindful of the way Jacopo had taken their own sister's dowry, Filippo began plans for setting aside a certain sum each month in order to provide a dowry to Maria. In thanks, Mrs. Martin offered to help out in Filippo's shops, and though he funded her living quarters and other needs at a higher rate than a salary could have done, she chose to give back in that small way. It helped Filippo to know someone looked after the shops as he made frequent trips in and around Italy to collect more products to sell.

On one such trip, Filippo befriended Giuseppe Norsa, co-owner with a brother of the Norsa Company, the second richest house among the Jews of Mantua, a city then under the control of the Hapsburgs of Austria. The Norsas funded a trip for Filippo to Venice to purchase pearls for sale in London as they had become quite a commodity. Once that deal was completed to everyone's satisfaction, with Filippo negotiating a price better than expected, he decided to visit some old friends in Livorno before returning to London.

On his third day there, a letter arrived from Raimondo Cocchi, his oldest friend in the city: "I wanted to warn you that a letter against you has been filed here. It is alleged that you sent a large number of banned books on a ship bound for Genoa, Livorno, Civitavecchia, Naples, and Messina for the purpose of infecting all of Italy. The matter is one for the Inquisition and may cause you some trouble. If it is untrue, have a good laugh at the story."

Filippo did laugh as he wrote Raimondo that it could not be true because he now "dealt in wines, because gentlemen replenish their wine cellars at much more frequent intervals than their libraries, since they prefer drinking to reading." Then he promptly forgot the joke, so busy was he in arranging for more products to ship back to his shops in London.

Before returning to London, Filippo stopped in Florence to see Chancellor Mazzini, a good friend of his brother Giuseppe's, at the Council of Eight. Filippo hoped to handle some business for his brother-in-law, who could not appear himself as he had been taken ill. The chancellor stared at Filippo for a moment.

"You are Filippo Mazzei, correct?" asked Mazzini.

"Yes," answered Filippo, "but this business concerns my brother-in-law—"

Mazzini cut him off by passing a sheet of paper across his desk. It demanded Filippo leave the state in exile over the charge of transporting banned books.

Immediately, Filippo went with Raimondo to the marshal of the Inquisition demanding an explanation. The marshal took the sentence of exile lightly, arguing that Filippo already resided in London, so why not simply return there quickly?

"This is a matter of honor. Could any gentleman face such a charge—and such a sentence—with equanimity, with calmness, with composure?" Filippo asked. "This is my home country and I must have the right, no matter how far I travel, to return where and when I choose."

Raimondo pulled Filippo away. "It is useless here. This man makes justice a mockery."

The two men left the office and devised the only plan available to them. Filippo would travel to Lucca, some fifty miles to the east of Florence and out of the magistrate's power, where

Filippo knew an oil merchant he had done business with ear-lier. Raimondo would stay in Florence to gather evidence to prove the charges false. His brother-in-law, Angiolo Tavanti, served as secretary to the marshal and could keep both men informed as the proceedings moved forward.

It took three months of letters back and forth between Filippo, Raimondo, and a host of their friends to find the truth. Meanwhile, Filippo also exchanged letters with his friends and associates in London, managing his shops from afar. To keep his businesses running, Filippo needed to travel to Naples for a con-tract, but knew his movements might be tracked. Feeling like a fugitive, which in fact he had become, Filippo slipped from city to city, meeting with powerful friends and gathering letters of support to present to the Inquisition. In Livorno, he received such a letter from Signor Giuseppe Aubert, and in Naples, where he stayed four months, he gathered support from Don Domen-ico la Leonessa, the son of the Duke of Matalona; the Marquis Acciaioli; and Sir William Hamilton, the British envoy.

Before Hamilton wrote Filippo his letter, he tried to con-vince the young man to return to his friends and businesses in England. "I advise you to ignore the insolent treatment you have received in your native country," Hamilton advised. "It will do no harm among Italian men whose opinion really matters. And it will be difficult to obtain justice in view of the inability of persons in power to admit their mistakes."

"As you love the country of your birth," Filippo responded, "I love mine and I cannot leave with my name clouded by con-troversy."

Understanding that his young friend's desire to clear his name stood paramount in his mind, Hamilton arranged for a meeting between Filippo and King Ferdinand IV, King of Naples and Sicily. Having come to the throne after the abdication of his father, Charles III of Spain, the fourteen-year-old Ferdinand had no real interest in governing, something the thirty-five-year-old Filippo had heard from many inside the court.

In fact, the Marquis Bernardo Tanucci, who had presented Filippo at court at the behest of Hamilton and had also raised the teenage king from childhood, admitted it to Filippo freely. "What would you expect? He's been brought up by a rascally priest." The two men shared a laugh at Tanucci's expense.

When they went in to dinner together so Filippo could meet the king, Filippo had an even better look at the immaturity of the young king. When Tanucci saw Filippo watching the king eat, he whispered, "He eats more at his age than any two grown men with hearty appetites. If we don't find ways to curb him, we'll have another Henry VIII on our hands."

"I won't hold a good appetite against a growing boy," Filippo whispered back. Observing how the king took delight in humiliating his servers, keeping them kneeling for an uncomfortable length of time and laughing at their discomfort, Filippo added, "But I do hope he learns to treat his courtiers with better respect as he grows."

"That is my next task," said Tanucci. "But first I will address my attention to your little matter. I will write a letter to the pope for the king to sign, and I will introduce you to other royals and those in high places from whom we can solicit letters."

Tanucci was as good as his word, presenting Filippo to many important people. With each lord and lady Filippo met, he engaged in conversation on topics of all kinds, from the proper education of children to whether the view of Capri from the sea ranked higher than the view of Constantinople from the strait of Bosphorous, always making himself welcome. He was becoming a favorite of dukes and other titled people in Italy and they rallied around to support his case. He humbly credited his popularity among the royals when he wrote to his sister, "In all circumstances I have acted in the same manner, and my behavior has been attributed more to modesty than to sound policy. I have never wished anyone to ask 'Why is Mazzei here?' but rather 'Why is Mazzei not here?'"

Finding some royals deeply intelligent and others deeply ignorant fed Filippo's distaste of the act of royal succession and fueled his later interest in supporting the colonists in their overthrow of King George III. In the meantime, Filippo decided to go to Rome to face the tribunal of the Inquisition himself, letters in hand—though Filippo would be without a passport, so if they chose to incarcerate him, he would be trapped.

Tanucci vetoed the plan instantly. "I should not take any chances in a country where the government seeks to make fools believe it is doing a pious work, when in reality, it is committing the worst wickedness."

Instead, Filippo returned to Florence with the letters Tanucci had gathered in his possession and presented them to the office of the marshal of the Inquisition, who sent word to "Do nothing. Everything is over." Thanks to the flood of letters from highly placed new friends and to Raimondo's investigations, they proved that the tale of trading in banned books came from a Roman priest, who, to escape punishment for crimes he had committed, fled to London. Many months before Filippo had refused a meeting with that priest, knowing his crimes, so the priest had fabricated the story that Filippo not only printed and distributed the banned books, but also had actually written many of them himself.

"This is by far the most ridiculous charge," Filippo said to Raimondo. "Any learned man knows these are the words of Voltaire and Rousseau."

"That is your problem, Filippo," Raimondo said. "You expect others to respect and to crave learning as you do when that is not the case among many men in power. They inherit their position and therefore have no need of earning it by reading."

While Filippo's case helped abolish the Inquisition in Tuscany, which disappeared within the year, the whole experience of injustice would stay with him for the rest of his life. It would build the foundation for a philosophy of justice for all and the need to separate church and state issues that would fuel his work on the Virginia plan for the U.S. Constitution.

In the midst of his victory over the arcane Inquisition, sad news came of another injustice Filippo felt powerless to solve. Days before his intended departure from Naples, Filippo received a desperate letter from his brother Giuseppe: "In the five years during which we have not seen each other, everything has happened to our dear mother that we predicted. She has been treated much worse by Jacopo than before your visit, and unless you come to her rescue with the funding that I cannot provide, she will be reduced to eating the grass that grows on the highways or she will die under the tyranny of an inhuman son."

Filippo journeyed immediately to his sister's home to learn more, and there he found his mother, who begged his forgiveness through tears. He hired a lawyer and brought a suit against his brother for the funds necessary to care for their mother. But Jacopo was wily as ever. Hearing he was to be put to trial, he sold his carriage, fired his servants, and leased out his properties in such a way as to allow him to plead poverty. Jacopo also hired friends to testify that his mother had never known more than a meager existence and so his funding had been sufficient. As the word of a woman was not taken as equally in court as the word of a man, the judge accepted Jacopo's defense and the case was closed.

The only solution for Filippo then was to return to his businesses in London to make enough money to send what his mother needed directly to his sister, who would use the money properly. Filippo would do this for the rest of his mother's life; when she died, he would continue sending money to his sister, as she had become a widow and she and her three children relied on his support.

On his way back to London, Filippo stopped in Pisa to meet with Grand Inquisitor Father Dini as the final step in his now-resolved case. It turned out Dini wanted to apologize and show him that it had all been settled.

"I have neither said nor done anything more than I have been ordered to do," Dini stated simply.

"Even if all these lies were true, this was never a case large enough for the Inquisition," Filippo countered.

"All our courts are subject to the court in Rome," Dini said, defending his position. "We are obliged to obey its orders blindly, without being permitted the privilege of making the least reflection on the subject ourselves."

Filippo made note of that excuse and wondered if there was any way to arrange a court to be truly fair to all and sundry, no matter their status in life.

Chapter Seven

BEFRIENDING FRANKLIN AND BUILDING A FORTUNE

Filippo returned to London, ready to build up his fortunes now that he had the care of his mother and sister to consider. Luckily, in his long absence, his friend Giuseppe Norsa had continued managing his shop with the help of an assistant Filippo had chosen before leaving the country. Norsa had done such a fine favor that the profits were strong enough to suggest opening another store in the Haymarket District, across the street from the Italian opera house. All things Italian were of great interest in London in the spring of 1767. Italian violinist Gaetano Pugnani led the orchestra at the opera house and intrigued music lovers by experimenting with a less curved bow and thicker strings. When Filippo met the maestro, Pugnani was in the middle of composing a comic opera, *Nanetta e Lubino,* which would debut in two years' time. The two men became friends in business and pleasure as they attended several local salons together on their free evenings.

Meanwhile, a letter from a friend in Florence, museum director Abbot Fontana, brought Filippo in direct contact with the American colonies in the person of their most famous citizen, Dr. Benjamin Franklin. And it was all because of a stove. Two stoves, in fact. The abbot had been ordered to obtain two Franklin stoves from Filippo for delivery to the Tuscan estate of Grand Duke Leopold II. While this commission would be financially lucrative for Filippo's shops, the true benefit came from gaining the friendship of such a renowned, learned, likeable man as Franklin.

When tasked with purchasing these stoves, Filippo researched and learned that many local artisans, not given to being mere copyists, often included their own changes to the models they made. Rather than risk buying copies that did not work well or would be called fakes upon placement in the duke's residence, Filippo decided to obtain a letter of introduction to Franklin to ask for his help in obtaining a proper stove.

Before asking for the letter, Filippo made sure to read some of Franklin's work in order to make intelligent conversation when they met. Franklin had been writing and publishing *Poor Richard's Almanack*, full of homespun advice such as "Early to bed and early to rise makes a man healthy, wealthy, and wise." In looking for something the two might have in common, Filippo found that Franklin had established one of the earliest medical facilities, the Pennsylvania Hospital in Philadelphia. Filippo was eager to discuss differences in medicine in Europe versus medicine in the colonies. He also knew that controversy followed Franklin since he had testified to the House of Commons against the Stamp Act only a few months earlier, answering over 170 questions without referring to notes. Parliament repealed the Stamp Act a month after Franklin's testimony, leaving little doubt that he was a masterful politician in the making.

Filippo found Franklin in his lodgings at the home of Mrs. Margaret Stevenson and her daughter, Polly, and being flattered by the request of a true example of his own handiwork, the American took Filippo from store to store in search of the purchase. Together the two strangers visited various craftsmen to find the best-made stoves. Instead, they found most manufacturers had made alterations in the design that Franklin did not endorse. Finally, they purchased two less-altered stoves and had them configured to Franklin's standards by a local artisan. The two men bonded over their shared love of detail and quality.

Franklin puttered around, tinkering with one of the stoves. "You'd think once a perfectly proper set of plans had been placed in their hands, your average artisan would simply follow them, understanding that the inventor had already tried these other ideas and found them wanting."

Filippo took a chance and teased his new friend. "When you invented this appliance, were you not tinkering with a plan already created by a craftsman?"

Franklin smiled. "Yes, but my changes made the thing better." Both men laughed as Franklin found an obstruction to the flue and pulled it out. "See?" he said, pointing to it. "My idea was to lengthen the path that the fire's fumes follow before they reach the chimney, allowing more heat to be extracted from the fumes."

Filippo watched as Franklin adjusted the flue and then worked on the metal panel that directed the flow of the fire's fumes, the baffle.

"*Now* it's a Franklin stove," the inventor announced as he stood back to admire his work.

"How is it that others can amend your design and still call them Franklin stoves?" Filippo asked. "It would seem to nullify the patent."

"Ah," Franklin sighed, "that is where I failed. Invention, experiments, expressing my thoughts in pithy little extemporanea…these are all my strengths. Considering the legal outcomes of these things is not. The deputy governor of Pennsylvania himself, George Thomas, made me an offer to patent my design, but I make it a point never to patent any of my designs or inventions."

"But why?"

"As we enjoy great advantages from the inventions of others, we should be glad of an opportunity to serve others by any invention of ours. And this we should do freely and generously."

Filippo liked that philosophy and added it to his own personal collection of growing ideas of what made a good life.

Together they shipped the two newly adjusted stoves to the Grand Duke Leopold, and over time other royals of Europe wrote requesting true Franklin stoves. The owner of the shop, who had watched Filippo and Franklin make their adjustments, sold more and more and even opened a new shop.

Meanwhile, the American and the Italian became friends over shared meals at Franklin's lodgings with Mrs. Stevenson. They discussed the differences between Americans and Europeans and why these differences were creating the agitation that kept making the news. Often they swapped books that had helped each man come to his own conclusions about which side to take in the many religious and political debates that were all the rage in London that year. Though Franklin was quite well read, Filippo enjoyed exposing him to Italian works not yet translated into English, including one of his favorites, Cesare Beccaria's essay *On Crimes and Punishments,* the book Filippo read after witnessing the Greek grocer hung in his own store.

"It is a masterwork of the Milan Enlightenment," Filippo said as he handed the leather-bound volume to Franklin, who, being a printer, studied the tooling of the leather and seemed to judge the book's contents by the quality of its cover.

"I found it a humane and wise treatise," Filippo declared.

Franklin ran his fingers along the binding of the book. "I will pay you a compliment I pay few men. I will read something you deem worthy because I sense you are a man who loves learning."

Through Franklin, Filippo met Thomas Adams of Virginia, another colonist living and doing business in London. "No relation to that *other* Adams family, the one from New England," Adams said when Franklin introduced them at a salon in the home of Mrs. Stevenson one Friday night. "While John and Samuel carry my surname, they are no relation to me, yet they are making Adams a name that causes eyebrows to raise and certain doors to be closed to me."

"You do not agree with their goals?" Filippo asked gently, deeply interested in the ideas floating around about the colonists' displeasure with King George.

"I do not agree with some of their more bombastic methods," Adams assured him. "And I worry what they will get up to while I am gone and how that will affect my business dealings here. Luckily, in the colonies I am more associated with my dear friend Mr. Thomas Jefferson, a young but deeply intelligent lawyer in my part of the colonies."

Adams had spent many nights in conversation with Jefferson, so his name, and his ideas, permeated much of his own conversation, making Filippo interested in meeting such a thinker one day.

In the meantime, with connections from both Franklin and Adams, Filippo expanded his import business by selling Italian foods to Americans as well as Londoners. Among the most popular items were Parmesan cheese, olive oils, wine, small sausages, anchovies, and farinaceous foods including dried polenta and pasta. Adams joked that much of this product went directly to Shadwell, Jefferson's father's home, where the younger Jefferson was becoming well known for his extravagant tastes. Between his business and personal dealings with Adams, Filippo came to know many other Virginians living in London and began to nurture the idea of visiting the colony some day.

His acquaintance with Americans deepened when, sadly, the house that stored his wares accidentally burned down. On Franklin's advice, Filippo had availed himself of the relatively new practice of insuring his business for £2,000, which proved prescient when the fire happened six months later. Filippo had the house connected to the storage facility rebuilt, and moved there to make business easier and because it was closer to the Americans living in London and to the docks from which his shipments came and went. Filippo began to imagine himself on one of those boats bound for the colonies in the same way he once imagined sailing to South America. This time, he sensed this feeling was more than the dream of a child wanting to impress his elders with riches untold. It was the desire of a man to live among other men he respected and valued.

"I thought I had found that here in London," Filippo confessed to Adams and Franklin one day over beer and sandwiches at a local pub.

"What changed your mind?" asked Adams.

"Many things," mused Filippo. "I've grown tired of royals."

"But as I hear it, you are their darling," Franklin said with a smile. "Look how they rescued you from the Inquisition."

"*You* are their darling, Ben," said Filippo with assurance. "It is all we hear wherever we go. Franklin said this. Franklin said that."

"Ah, well, I could say the same of you," Franklin said. "You could rewrite Milton and they would still love you."

"Fine," admitted Filippo. "I have not grown tired of some royals, those who don't abuse their power and who know their blessings, like the Grand Duke Leopold. But living here under King George…"

"You mean King Bute," joked Franklin, referring to John Stuart, the third Earl of Bute and prime minister, who had raised the current king from boyhood. Many blamed Bute for creating a man who could not see the harm his decisions caused among his subjects, both in the colonies and at home in England.

"The only decent thing this king has ever done," began Adams, "was to declare himself a true Englishman and thereby distance himself from those nasty German forebears."

"I believe, if rumors prove true, his not taking a mistress is worthy of praise," added Filippo, always ready to see the good in someone. "However, that makes him a moral man, but his decisions have not made him a moral king."

"So come with us back to the colonies," Franklin said. "We have no aristocracy there. The eyes of the people are not dazzled by the splendor of the throne."

"Granted, nothing is perfect," admitted Adams, "but the head of each family votes in our local elections and can even run for local office. Being out of sight of the king allows us to keep only the English laws we like, those that fit our needs."

"And to invent the rest?" Filippo asked with a sly smile, nodding toward Franklin, who had a gleam in his eye.

"Come invent a new world with us," Franklin said. "How many times in a life does a man have such a chance?"

A week later, as Filippo dined with another friend, Anthony Chamier, the arguments against the move were nearly as strong.

"I never expected such a resolution from a man of sense as you are," said Chamier over the after-dinner hot chocolate drink.

"You will leave a place where you have so great a number of excellent friends that no foreigner ever had in order to go to a country, where, if you break a chair, you will find nobody to mend it for you."

"I have made friends here among strangers. Why shouldn't I do the same there?"

"You have a certain talent for making friends, but it seems you have also a talent for leaving them. I wish, at least, that the little dirty tricking knavery of America may prove less interruption to your comforts of life than the plain downright roguery of this country."

"I understand that no country is perfect," admitted Filippo. "Traditions can hold back progress, inherited lands can confound commerce…I've seen it both in Tuscany and here, in this supposed land of free men. This new land offers me a chance to make tradition, to make history. If I don't go now, I'll regret it later in life, when it will be too late to try."

Deciding to take a chance on the colonies, Filippo had settled his financial affairs with all his suppliers and customers within three months, but needed advice on how to handle the matter of his promised care to Mrs. Martin and her now-seventeen-year-old daughter, Maria.

"Take them with you," advised Franklin.

"The young Maria will make a much better marriage in Virginia than here in London," Adams said. "Once you settle into your estates you will be a landed man, and that will make her all the more enticing."

"The best thing I can do for her father is to make sure she weds well," said Filippo. Then he changed the subject. "Tell me again about Williamsburg. Why is it the best place to be in Virginia?"

Adams described the city, founded in 1633 as a safe haven for settlers after the war that followed the Indian Massacre of 1622. A lush area, good for growing. First called Middle Plantation based on its originally intended purpose, the city had grown to include, in 1693, the premier university, William and Mary, the second one built and funded in the colonies, named after King William III and Queen Mary II.

"John Adams, when you meet him, will tell you Harvard is the better of the two," Franklin said with a nod across the table to Adams. "But Jefferson and I know the difference. Harvard men, like John Adams, are far too narrow in their thinking."

"You belong in Virginia," affirmed Adams.

Before he could travel to the colonies, Filippo had to return to Tuscany to collect tools particular to the work of a vineyard, which he planned to establish in the red, rich soil Adams promised him. Certain specially shaped spades, billhooks, and sickles were made only in Italy. Filippo also planned to hire a group of vineyard workers to come with him. Wine would be a new commodity in that new world and Filippo could not risk its care to inexperienced hands.

He had another reason to recruit the peasants. He knew from separate conversations with Adams, who approved of the idea, and Franklin, who did not, that the farmers in Virginia had become quite reliant on enslaved Africans for labor. Filippo agreed with Franklin and thought he might make some contribution to change that attitude in Virginia by the hiring of peasants as indentured servants, a system that had gone out of favor in the colonies.

Filippo took the trip back to Tuscany with Mrs. Martin, Maria, and Adams's friend Samuel Griffin, also from Virginia, who wanted to see more of Europe before heading home with Filippo's group. The foursome took a coach from Lyons to Paris and the three hundred-mile journey took a swift five days, with meals and overnight stays provided at the price of four louis per person. In each city Griffin and the ladies took in the sites while Filippo tended to business, except in Tuscany, where they were all granted an audience with the grand duke, who wished to thank Filippo in person for acquiring the stoves for him. That had made the duke the first royal on the continent to have such innovative technology installed in his palace.

"It is I who must thank you, sovereign," said Filippo bowing. "By your hand I made the acquaintance of Benjamin Franklin and from him I acquired the desire to see this new world for myself."

Together the men discussed how Filippo's settling in Virginia could be advantageous to the grand duke in terms of profits from the imports and exports they could arrange. The duke had also been soliciting interest from some of his local peasants to see which of his skilled men would be interested in traveling with Filippo.

"A man who does not wish to move will not do his best work in his new situation," he advised.

Filippo spent the next few weeks meeting with men interested in joining him in the colonies. Some deeply feared the idea, superstitiously believing rumors that raged about how "the stars fall from the sky and burn laborers in the fields" there.

Filippo tried to assuage these fears, explaining, "Those are merely meteors which appear like comets falling from the sky and which the common people call stars," but his explanations were not always accepted.

Once one or two men signed on, it became easier to recruit others. One of the first, and most important due to his talents, was Antonio Giannini, twenty-six, a skilled gardener, vigneron, and grafter of vines who had come from near Lucca with his wife, Maria Domenica Modena, and their two-year-old daughter, Maria Caterina. Then Maria's brother Francis Modena signed on for the journey, too, along with another man who could serve as a main gardener, Giovannini da Prato.

A fifteen-year-old boy, Giovanni Fabbroni, appeared one day with a seventeen-year-old friend, both interested in joining Filippo's employ, but Filippo was unimpressed with the older of the two and offered employment only to Fabbroni. Sadly, Fabbroni turned him down out of loyalty to his older friend. Then twenty-year-old Vincenzo Rossi came from a nearby town and begged Filippo for the chance. Filippo tested him with the meteor rumors, but they were not as strong in Rossi as the desire to better his situation.

"Here I can never be more than my father, a farmhand. In America, as I am told, I can own my own farm," Rossi said.

Filippo consulted with the grand duke on all his hires, which turned out to be quite helpful, especially in the case of one man from Comeana. The duke quickly identified the man as "the greatest rascal and thief in the duchy."

"But in America, he would not be able to steal," said Filippo.

"Oh, he would steal all right," responded the duke. "Although there would be no harm done, even were they to hang him, he would spoil all your other men and would cause you trouble instead of being useful."

Filippo took the grand duke's advice and thanked him for it.

When finally all ten men had been agreed upon, Filippo welcomed them warmly to this shared adventure. The men all signed contracts of indenture, offering five years of labor in exchange for room and board and a parcel of land granted at the end of their service. Most would work on the vineyards and farm. Filippo hired only one, a tailor from Piedmont, to keep all his workers clothed and to serve as the steward of the home Filippo would build.

With their business completed, the grand duke gave Filippo one final warning that he was making the move during a particularly tumultuous time in the colonies. Correspondence between royals all over Europe crackled with worry about how King George handled the colonies, and what other colonies belonging to other empires might learn from the protests then going on in America. Due to Filippo's friendships with Franklin and Adams, and the correspondence he himself had begun with Thomas Jefferson over questions of farming in Virginia, Filippo knew much about the thoughts of the colonists.

"This business with the tea imports to Boston is only the beginning," Filippo told the grand duke. "Second and third boats loaded with tea were not even allowed to dock in Philadelphia and New York."

"But for it to come to war?"

"According to Franklin, the colonists are convinced Parliament will not permit arms to be sent against them and Parliament is convinced the colonists will not have the courage to fight their own troops. He is in a position to know these thoughts as he has spoken in person with men of both continents. In my opinion, such mutual misconceptions cannot lead to anything other than war."

"And you still want to be there? Now?" the grand duke said with a smile.

"How many times in a life does a man have such a chance?" Filippo smiled back.

Chapter Eight

BEFRIENDING JEFFERSON IN VIRGINIA AND BUILDING A "SOCIETY TO OUR TASTE"

On September 2, 1773, the frigate *Triumph,* a three-mast ship, sailed from Livorno with Filippo, Mrs. Martin, Maria, and ten indentured peasants aboard, along with a hold full of cuttings, seeds, small animals, silkworms to raise for the production of silk, and those particular tools Filippo had gathered in Tuscany. On days when the sea was calm, Maria stood on the deck with Filippo, looking out over the horizon and either imagining her future or remembering her past, as Filippo did. Mrs. Martin preferred to stay below deck as the rocking motion seemed less intense there.

As he looked out across the water, Filippo heard echoes in his head, words from those who had truly loved him. He heard his nonno say, "*It is a fact of life that a mama will often love her firstborn son best…I was the third son, too. I know that fighting against what is true is a waste of time. But that doesn't mean you stop. It means you double your efforts because someone, someday will see the truth in you.*"

He heard his uncle, on the day he tried to join Giuseppe in the monastery, say, *"Giuseppe belongs here. You belong in school. That is the way of the world. Accept it or you will never survive."*

He heard his friend David, after Filippo helped heal his mother, say, *"Take it one day at a time. A path will become clear. And you will know it is the one to follow."*

In the middle of his reveries, Maria tapped Filippo on the wrist. "Can it be true? Is there really something out there? How can you know if you have never seen it?"

"I have friends who have," he answered softly.

"Can you trust them?"

"In my life I have found that the friends you cultivate can be more family…than family," he responded, thinking sadly of Jacopo, but then remembered the generosity of Domenico and Vincenzo in Livorno; Raimondo and Dr. Cocchi; Dr. Salinas; Franklin; and Adams, who had promised to sell Filippo some prime land next to his in Williamsburg. He had not yet truly realized how much his friendships had enriched his life until Maria posed the question.

Maria, obviously thinking of what a good friend Filippo had been—and was still being—to her late father, smiled and said, "I have found this as well."

As they watched the waves crash against the side of the boat, deep in their individual thoughts, they heard the song of the captain's canaries. The beautiful birds sang every morning.

"Am I mistaken or today there is more lilt in their tones?" Maria asked.

"They are breathing the air of their native land," answered Filippo, who, upon hearing the tones, focused his view farther across the horizon, where he saw vague beginnings of the islands of Madeira. He pointed it out to Maria.

"Is that America?" she asked anxiously.

"We have not traveled nearly long enough to reach America," Filippo said gently. "These are the Madeira Islands, off the coast of Morocco. Beautiful, yes, but not our destination just yet. That will be even more beautiful."

"How do you know if you have never seen it?" Maria asked again, teasingly.

In late November the *Triumph* docked at Trebell's Landing and Burwell's Ferry, on the James River about four miles from Williamsburg. Filippo and his party—which the captain had dubbed "Filippo's ark" as it included such a combination of people, animals, and plants as to constitute the beginning of a new Eden—disembarked. Francis Eppes VI, whose wife was Thomas Jefferson's sister-in-law, met them with carriages and took Filippo, Mrs. Martin, and Maria to his home for a respite before moving on to Thomas Adams's promised land.

"We are pleased to have you," Eppes said as the group stepped down from their carriages.

The ladies tried to dust off their dresses by tapping them with their fans, but the ride across red dirt roads had been quite dry and the carriages created a cloud as they drove.

"My wife is ever so eager to make your acquaintance," Eppes insisted.

"In our traveling clothes?" asked a mortified Mrs. Martin, looking around to see if Mrs. Eppes had come outside.

"We will make your introductions at dinner. There will be plenty of time to freshen up before then," Eppes assured the party as the ladies were quickly ushered inside.

The two men shook hands.

"How can I repay you for your kind welcome?" Filippo asked.

"From what my brother-in-law wrote me, your conversation at the table will be enough!" said Eppes.

"Perhaps we can also find some business to transact that will allow me to pay back your kindness and make our acquaintance mutually beneficial for years to come," Filippo said as plans already began whirling around in his head.

At Eppes's home, several leaders of Williamsburg came to meet their newest countryman. Though they came from all around the colony, they were conveniently in the capital city for an assembly meeting that had ended a day earlier. Having been told through correspondence with Jefferson that Filippo would be an important new man in agriculture for their region, and informed by Eppes that his ship had arrived, many important Virginians stayed in town a few days longer to make Filippo's acquaintance over a meal at Eppes's home. George Washington, who owned a plantation called Mount Vernon some 140 miles to the north, came to see him, as did George Wythe, Jefferson's lawyer and a local to Williamsburg. A twenty-two-year-old friend and neighbor of Jefferson's, James Madison, spoke excitedly of the revolutionary activities that angered his own father but excited him, and Thomas Adams came with his brother Richard, who wanted to sample the wines Filippo had brought on the ship for possible sale in his own stores.

All of the callers shared Filippo's enthusiasm for the making—and drinking—of wine, knowing that in 1768, Virginians exported from Britain a little more than thirteen tons of wine from overseas, and another 78,264 from other North American colonies. But a few warned him that Virginia soil had been tried and so far unproven to be suitable. They told

Filippo the story of Frenchman Andrew Estave, designated the winemaker and viticulturist for Virginia by the General Assembly in 1770. Estave had lived in the colony only two years, studied the soil, cultivated wild grapes, and promised to make "good merchantable Wine in four years from the seating and planting of the Vineyard."

"Like all before him, he failed," Washington explained on his visit. "Estave thought his stocks of European grapes too fragile for the climate."

Filippo smiled. "I would say Frenchmen are too fragile for the climate. I have come with good, solid Roman stock."

That brought a round of laughter as the men drank their locally made Madeira, which Washington claimed relieved the heat of summer and warmed the chilled blood and the bitter cold of winter.

All these new associates also wondered what Filippo thought of the city. Having seen some of the greatest cities of the old world, Filippo secretly thought Williamsburg to be no more than a mere township, not a proper city at all. Still, he politely complimented all that they had created, particularly the college and the local hospital he had heard so much about from Jefferson's letters. Filippo's own natural enthusiasm for the move made him convinced that soon the area would rival any city in Europe, and he had seen several.

Before Filippo and his entourage could travel to the land Thomas Adams was hoping he would buy to begin his vineyard, Filippo convinced several local farmers to take grain they were planning to ship to the sugar islands and instead send it on to Livorno, a port no Virginian ship had ever considered. To illustrate his belief in the profit that could be made between Virginia and Livorno, and all of Tuscany, Filippo funded his own ship of new-world products to be sent back under the command of Captain Woodford, a fellow recommended to him by Adams. As a thank you to the grand duke, the ship contained a gift to the monarch of three fallow deer, two males and a female, that Filippo found elegant and beautiful due to the hue of their skin. He also sent along three birds that did not exist in Tuscany, one of them the reddest cardinal he could find, as well as a rattlesnake and several barrels of the finest flour from a mill owned and operated by another new local friend, John Banister.

Filippo took the time to study the five thousand local acres he had been granted by the Virginia Assembly, but found the soil unsuitable for a vineyard and had to decline. Adams himself was moving to Augusta County, over two hundred miles inland from Williamsburg. He assured Filippo that the soil there would be more to his liking, so the little caravan of Italians headed west with Adams with the intention of establishing the first vineyard in North America—but a chance stop for dinner at Monticello changed everything.

The friendship that was to last a lifetime began as Adams's carriages rode up the grand driveway of Monticello and Filippo saw at a glance how much Jefferson esteemed all things Italian. The neoclassical design of the main home came from principles described by Italian Renaissance architect Andrea Palladio.

"How do you know that?" Adams asked Filippo as they drove.

"I have read Palladio's *Four Books of Architecture,* both as a student and later, when I moved to London and I used the English version to help me learn the language," Filippo answered. "Among all the architects in Europe, Palladio is considered the most influential individual in the history of architecture. His precepts are unforgettable." Filippo felt the pride of his homeland as he took in the grandeur of the four columns and the center rotunda. "To see my culture echoed in this new land—"

"It means you belong here, my friend," said Adams.

More than the echo of Italian architecture, Filippo felt at home the moment the thirty-two-year-old Jefferson stepped out the front portico, all six-feet-two inches of him, and greeted them in Italian, though he mispronounced "*Ciao*," saying it phonetically as "Siow."

For an instant Filippo did not know how to respond. To correct his host seemed disrespectful, but to allow him to continue uncorrected could cause embarrassment later.

Jefferson clearly saw the confusion on Filippo's face and switched to English. "You must excuse my pronunciation, sir," began Jefferson. "Having only read the language up until now, I have never heard the words spoken. I hope I have caused no offense."

"No offense taken at all," promised Filippo immediately in English.

"The great Jefferson has made a mistake?" laughed Adams heartily. "I *knew* Filippo would be an asset to the colonies!"

Filippo switched to Italian to say "Hello, and thank you," pronouncing each word slowly so that Jefferson could take note, which he clearly did. "Thank you for offering such generous hospitality in such an elegant home."

Jefferson basked in the compliment to his pride and joy. "I have often said to others who live in the vicinity that Italy is a field where the inhabitants of the southern states may see much to copy in agriculture," he said, again exercising his Italian.

Adams laughed heartily. "Would anyone care to translate or shall I retire to my rooms and allow you two to continue the lessons?"

"We shall all retire," Jefferson said, "after our guest has done me one more favor."

"Anything," said Filippo.

"May you please allow me to hear the name of my home pronounced by a native?" Jefferson asked.

"Of course," said Filippo as he stood on the portico admiring the view of the main gardens and the mountains beyond. Then he said Monticello phonetically as *Mon-ti-chel-lo*. "Little mount."

"Ah," Jefferson noted. "Your 'ce' is pronounced 'ch.' I shall remember that. Italian is such a delightful language, but I fear learning it has confounded my French and Spanish."

Then Filippo watched warmly as Jefferson himself looked out over his land and said for the first time, "Monticello."

As it had been such a long trip, the men all retired to their rooms with Jefferson extracting a promise that Filippo would rise early and join him on his morning rounds. So before breakfast, and before Filippo had the chance to meet the lady of the house, Martha Jefferson, the two men set out on foot across leaf-strewn paths to see what Jefferson had built. Walking up and down the mountain was made easier by the level roundabouts and rising connecting roads Jefferson had designed. Even this early in the day, enslaved men were already out in some areas, harvesting trees and dragging them back to workshops to create planks and cabinets and other articles for use on the plantation, or for sale. Material for work and products for sale came to and from Monticello via the Rivanna River, which the two men approached on one of the paths.

"*Che bella vista,*" said Filippo quietly, not wanting to disturb the quiet of the early morning.

"It's why I wanted to own this land, not merely to inherit my father's land next door," said Jefferson, also in a low voice.

Together the two men followed the river and split off to walk a bit of the Shadwell property. Though the home had burned in 1770, Jefferson wanted to check how production was going at the gristmill there. Along the way they passed through the flatter land of Monticello, at the base of the mountain, in an area named Tufton Farm, where they cultivated most of the wheat.

"My father forewent tobacco for wheat several years ago," Jefferson explained, "influenced by Washington, who fancies himself a great farmer, though I'm convinced he's a better surveyor."

"But I thought tobacco to be the darling crop of Europe," said Filippo.

"The problem is, tobacco can wear out your soil if you are not careful about its cultivation. And…at this time in our relations to our mother country," Jefferson said, "wheat exports do not require the same financial entanglements with English merchants, so many of my neighbors have moved away from tobacco."

"But if my eyes do not deceive, you have not yet made that move, my new friend," said Filippo.

"Many of the English merchants have begun to sell tobacco at a price too low to suit the planters in Virginia in order to break our ability to…dare I say it…foment rebellion. But my connections still pay me well, and being newly married, my first obligation is to provide for my wife a lifestyle to which she has become accustomed."

"Perhaps the merchants were told what I was told—that New England is the center of the rebellion," Filippo said.

"That's what John and Sam Adams want you to think," said Jefferson. "They may have a corner on the rhetoric, but we have the funds to support such an…adventure."

Filippo could tell Jefferson was feeling him out, to see which side Filippo would take since he came from a comfortable situation in England.

"I believe in freedom," Filippo stated in as straightforward a manner as possible. "I have seen too much of those in power dictating how those in poorer circumstances must live."

"Then we are in agreement," said Jefferson, offering his hand. "Wonderful."

As Filippo shook hands, he noted the small wooden cabins that dotted the edges of the field, enough to house the individual enslaved families he saw already at work, finishing the planting of soft red winter wheat seeds. Filippo knew he would have to resolve his thoughts about enslaved labor if he was going to succeed both professionally and personally in this community, so he was happy to see that Jefferson also employed some paid labor and some indentured servants, and hoped that his own use of those forms of labor exclusively might prove an example for his new friend. But this was not yet the time to broach such a deep subject.

As they walked, Jefferson talked at length. Filippo could tell he enjoyed conversing in this new language, and Filippo enjoyed the telling, so he listened intently. Jefferson described his first serious study of the Italian language, around 1764, when he purchased an Italian-English dictionary and three more historical works in Italian, one of which was the complete works of Niccolò Machiavelli and the other the copy of Palladio's *Four Books of Architecture* in the original Italian. Palladio's account of his most famous structure, the Villa Rotunda near Vicenza, so enthralled Jefferson that he had to sharpen his linguistics in order to understand how to bring that style to Virginia. Jefferson flipped through his journal until he found a quote he wanted to share from the famed architect: "We must contrive a building in such a manner that the finest and most noble parts of it be the most exposed to public view, and the less agreeable disposed in by places, and removed from sight as much as possible."

"Why the intense interest in a country you have yet to see?" Filippo asked.

"I could ask the same of you, my friend," observed Jefferson. "Something about my country lured you in. For me, Roman taste, genius, and magnificence excite ideas in me, and I know I will see Italy someday."

As Jefferson's linguistic skills grew, he had begun to fill the pages of his commonplace book with extracts from well-loved Italian poems. As the men ascended another small hill, they debated the talents of Virgil, Filippo's favorite poet, against Aeschylus, currently Jefferson's favorite.

"Having just come off a long sea voyage," Filippo said in preface, "I know the truth in Virgil's 'Storm.'" He recited to the trees, *"Now one heard the cries of men and screech of ropes in rigging. Suddenly, when the stormcloud whipped away clear sky and daylight from the Teucrians' eyes, and gloom of night leaned on the open sea. It thundered from all quarters, as it lightened flash on flash through heaven."*

"I feel the power of the sea," agreed Jefferson, "but with Aeschylus I feel the power of the heart." Then he recited in a much quieter voice, *"Even in our sleep, pain which cannot forget, falls drop by drop upon the heart, until, in our own despair, against our will, comes wisdom, through the awful grace of God."*

"Granted, it gives me shivers," said Filippo. "For such a young man, with so much to look forward to—new wife, new home, new ideas to make them both more enjoyable than they already are—it seems an odd poem on which to settle."

Jefferson took that thought in and pondered it silently as they crossed over into land owned by Edward Carter, a poorer neighbor of Jefferson's. Carter was hoping to sell his four-hundred-acre farm and move inland, where he could afford a larger tract to accommodate his twelve children.

"You have brought me here for a reason other than to debate the merits of our favorite poets," said Filippo with a smile.

"Perhaps," said Jefferson. "I love this land and intend to live out my life here, but without society, and a society to our taste, men are never contented. So buy this land and we can build a society to our taste. The young Madison will inherit land but a day's drive away and, as I understand it, you and he have already met."

"I have yet to see Mr. Adams's land in Augusta County."

"Albemarle County soil is far more fertile for vines than anywhere else in the colony."

"How do you know, since no one else has yet tried to cultivate wine in any of the colonies?"

Jefferson admitted no one could know for sure what soil would be best, but he said he thought most wine drinkers, and therefore most customers, were collected here in Albemarle. "Besides, is it not clear that I am deeply interested the agricultural prospects of Virginia? If you live beside me, I may watch this experiment in the cultivation of wine—and the almonds and olives and other Mediterranean plants you have brought—from a front-row seat."

More and more amazed at how two men born in countries so far from each other, into such seemingly different families and cultures, could share so much in common, Filippo swayed closer to Jefferson's plan. When the Virginian threw in a large number of his own acres to add to Filippo's holdings, he couldn't help but agree. Neighbors they would be.

Chapter Nine

FOUNDING A FARM AND FOMENTING REBELLION

As they walked back toward the main house, Jefferson turned the conversation back to his many agricultural innovations and experiments.

Filippo was in awe. "All your fields and gardens…look so green and fresh, even as winter descends. How is it possible to provide so much water atop such a mountain?"

Eager to see his ideas incorporated into the eventual building of Filippo's new home next door, Jefferson described his cistern system. Filippo could see how Jefferson designed the two terraces that flanked the main house for the purpose of collecting water into the matching cisterns on each side.

"Even the roof acts to collect all that falls," Filippo said as he noticed the way the gutters gathered and funneled even the gentle early morning rain that had begun to fall into the cisterns below the deck.

"Exactly! I collect nearly…six hundred gallons per rain day," Jefferson said, consulting his calculations recorded in the diary he carried with him everywhere.

Returning to the main home after such a monumental morning, the new friends took one last moment to admire Jefferson's cooling system, based on ancient temperature-control techniques such as ground-cooled air and heated floors, which Jefferson had read about in Roman and Renaissance texts. Monticello's central hall windows were designed to allow a current of cooling air to pass through the house so the octagonal cupola could draw hot air up and away.

When they turned the corner to the dining room, they found everyone up and at breakfast, including Adams, who took one look at the twinkle in Jefferson's eye and said, "I see by your expression that you have taken him away from me. I knew you would do that."

"You said I would love Virginia, and I do," Filippo reminded Adams.

"I meant you'd love Williamsburg," Adams shot back. "The city, the hospital, the university…living in the political capital of the colony."

"There will be a university here as well," said Jefferson.

"When?" asked Adams.

"Whenever I get around to starting one," Jefferson barked back. "And when I do, you can be sure Italian will be one of the main languages studied."

"Thomas," Martha began, "it is unseemly to disagree with a guest."

"Of course, my dear," Jefferson quickly agreed as he approached his young wife and kissed her hand in the European manner.

Martha Jefferson had a height that did not match her husband's, but came close enough to keep her from feeling too diminutive when standing beside him. Her auburn hair complemented his sandy red mane and his hazel-blue eyes. Filippo couldn't help but feel they made a lovely couple, though the twenty-three-year-old Martha carried with her a bit of the melancholy Filippo had noticed in other women. While occupied with making her guests comfortable, Martha also kept an eye on her infant daughter. Patsy sat in a high chair between the seats designated for her parents as an attendant put an empty plate on a shelf concealed by a paneled door that ran alongside the fireplace. When the attending slave closed the door and opened it again, a covered dish appeared, hot and steaming from the oven.

"How is that possible?" Filippo asked in amazement.

Jefferson smiled. "It is something all my first-time guests remark upon—and they are particularly amazed when at dinner an empty wine bottle goes in and a new and never-opened bottle appears. I call it a dumbwaiter. The panel conceals a narrow dumbwaiter that descends to the basement. A servant, waiting in the basement, pulls the dumbwaiter down, removes the empty plate—or bottle—inserts a fresh one and sends it up to me in a matter of seconds."

Filippo found the explanation fascinating, but not nearly as fascinating as the fact that the attendant managing the dumbwaiter looked far too much like Mrs. Jefferson for coincidence to be the cause.

Later, as they waited for coffee in the library and the two guests found themselves alone, Adams explained that the female servant was Sally Hemings, the half sister of the mistress of the house, born into slavery as the illegitimate child of Martha's father, John Wayles, and an enslaved woman. The information had become common knowledge upon Wayles's death when his will mentioned Sally's mother, Betty Hemings, and the six children she had birthed for him, and insisted they could never be sold away from each other.

"It's proof she was his mistress and not merely his slave," said Adams, shaking his head. "Jefferson inherited the lot when Wayles died, 11,000 acres of quality farmland and all his slaves, including Sally, her two sisters, and three brothers, who are all employed on the place."

"Employed?" Filippo questioned.

"In that they learn crafts they can use on their days off to earn their own money," explained Adams, not realizing that Filippo understood that aspect of the culture, but still did not agree with it. The whole conversation fueled Filippo's discomfort with the idea of chattel slavery. When another enslaved person with a complexion nearly as light as Filippo's own olive skin brought the coffee, he had a hard time looking in her eyes, but made himself do so in order to show as much respect as was possible under the circumstances. He stood up and browsed the shelves to distract himself, happy to find Jefferson's copies of both Dante's *Divine Comedy* and Machiavelli's *The Prince*.

The mood finally lifted as Jefferson entered the library, which clearly served as his sanctuary in such a busy life. Filippo instantly sensed the peace that came over his host as he walked into the room, eager to share his collection.

"I see you found the Italian section," Jefferson said.

"How appropriate," Adams commented.

"What do you think of Machiavelli?" asked Filippo.

"I think I do not ever intend to be a prince, or a king, so the advice is of no value to me," Jefferson smiled. "But it does help me evaluate the behavior of our current king, and—"

"And find him wanting?" Filippo completed the thought they all shared.

"Careful," Adams warned. "That kind of talk is considered treasonous."

"Many of these books discuss ideas that could be considered treasonous," Filippo noted as he ran his finger over the leather bindings on one of the shelves. He paused and reread the title of one book twice before pulling it from the shelf.

"You have read the Quran?" Filippo asked his host.

"I have," said Jefferson. "I have read many tracts on many religions in a search to find what is true."

"That is a search many have gone on without finding an answer," said Filippo. "Have you yet found one?"

Jefferson thought for a moment before answering. "I think, perhaps, there is no answer, certainly none that anyone can prove or it should not be called having faith. But I also think this search is worthy of man. Franklin and I have had this discussion often across our letters and I think we both agree that Deism is the only philosophy that makes sense for an intellectual."

"So you believe in nothing?" Filippo prodded.

"I believe there was a creator, for all of this could not be possible as accident. But I believe once he completed his creation he had no need to stay and watch how we steward it. So for me, prayer—as in the chanting prewritten phrases in a prescribed community building—has no purpose. I pray, rather say I meditate, as I ride through his creation."

This was yet another conundrum Filippo found in the personality of his new friend. To have been blessed with so much and not be able to be grateful to the one who gave it seemed an empty idea to Filippo. But it also seemed to be another topic of conversation that should wait until the two of them became closer, which Filippo felt was inevitable now that they would be neighbors.

Instead, Filippo turned the conversation to his travels in Turkey, highlighting the religious people he met there, and found time to mention his brother Giuseppe, the Capuchin monk, in an effort to insinuate his own philosophy concerning religion without offending his host by more blatantly disagreeing with his position. It would be a conversation they would continue over time while helping settle the question for the nation they helped found. As a microcosm of their future citizens, they helped decide the point that religion is personal and should not be dictated by government.

For now, this discussion allowed Jefferson to reflect on how much the two men had in common and how jealous Jefferson was of Filippo having seen places he had only read about. "I intend to see Europe someday," Jefferson declared. "If they'll have me, considering their opinion of our ideas of self-government."

Once pleasantries were over, it was time to get down to business once again. Adams had to return to his own lands, sans Filippo, and he took his leave sadly.

"I had hoped that we could become good friends," Adams said. "But perhaps it is still possible?"

Filippo smiled as he shook Adams's hand. "We already are. You have brought me to my new home and I will be forever in your debt."

Then he and Jefferson got down to business. They sent word to Eppes to send on Filippo's workers but to hold off bringing Mrs. Martin and Maria until a place was made for them. Then Jefferson took Filippo on a more extensive tour of how Monticello worked. This time they went down to Mulberry Row, the center of work and domestic life for dozens of people: free whites, free blacks, indentured servants, and enslaved people. It was populated by more than twenty dwellings—for both black and white workers, Filippo was glad to see—plus woodworking and ironworking shops, a brewery, dairy, smokehouse, wash house, and stable.

It is a city unto itself, Filippo thought.

As they walked down the row, Jefferson introduced Filippo to some of the artisans and Filippo took care to keep track of which were enslaved men, which were indentured, and which were free. It was a daunting task. He was happy to see that many remained in their family units, working together, though Filippo knew they would rather be toiling for their own benefit.

Ursula and George Granger lived in the first dwelling they visited, along with their son, Isaac, whom Jefferson praised for manning the tinsmithing operation so well. Next door, Richard Richardson served as brickmason, plasterer, and overseer. Jefferson complimented Isaac's work and admitted that often, when the crops did not bring the profit that they could, the other products these men and women created kept the plantation finances afloat. Outside profit also came from John Hemings, who ran the cabinetmaking shop, called the joinery. Beside that building was George Bradby, a free black man living with his enslaved wife, Jenny, while working for Jefferson to earn enough to buy her freedom. Filippo had the sense that Jefferson, who was oddly shy for being such a leader, was more comfortable among technological gadgets than he was among people. His eyes lit up as he showed Filippo the flying shuttle loom and a spinning jenny, which, though mechanical, had to be operated by skilled technicians, black and white.

"To be independent for the comforts of life," Jefferson said, "we must fabricate them ourselves."

"Ah, ingenious," remarked Filippo. "You are speaking of America's need to develop manufacturing, a truth you have clearly learned on the microscale of this plantation."

~

In ten days' time Filippo's workers arrived from Eppes's farm and began the task of deforesting his land and planting the vines they had brought from Tuscany. Even the tailor found work immediately from Jefferson, who fell in love with Filippo's hunting coat and paid the tailor for a copy. Soon others in the neighborhood asked for the same, which was a boon for the indentured workman, as the contract he had signed with Filippo allowed the tailor to keep the profits from any work outside of that done for Filippo and his men. Jefferson instantly fascinated the contingent of Italian peasants with his ability to speak their native language, while his immediate attraction to the particular tools of their trade led to having them copied in his ironworks and sold locally.

While the workers cleared the area intended for the main house, Filippo chose the name Colle, in honor of the area in Tuscany where he was born, Colle di Val d'Elsa. The men lived on Mulberry Row and Filippo stayed on as a guest at Monticello while the workers built his home. Jefferson so enjoyed the prospect of new building and helping Filippo make all the architectural decisions necessary for those new buildings that for a while, their days fell into a pattern. They supervised workmen on both plantations by day, and at dinners with multiple other local guests, they all discussed the day's events, both there in Albemarle County and across the colonies, based on whichever letters they had received that day from friends in other areas. Together, they composed responses, enjoying the act of collaborating on the writing and editing each other as they went along. He and Jefferson shared the recommendation of which books to read to enlighten them on the issues of liberty and proper government. A typical night would find Filippo defending Machiavelli, while Jefferson defended John Locke's theory of natural rights to help provide a reason for revolution.

"But Machiavelli is not advocating this kind of government," Filippo said one night over after-dinner hot chocolate. "He is simply saying this is *how* things are done, not how they *should* be done."

"Yes," agreed Jefferson, "but if that is how they are done, the author offers no suggestions on how to stop that from being the way things are done. Locke advocates the idea that government is meant to secure and protect the God-given inalienable natural rights of the people."

During these evening debates Filippo had the chance to recommend the same book to Jefferson that he had shared with Franklin, Cesare Beccaria's *On Crimes and Punishments*. Often other local leaders dined with them, sometimes as many as twenty or thirty at a time, and Filippo shared this book and his ideas with all his new friends in the colonies, including John Adams by written correspondence, and it shaped their ideas of law, liberty, and society as they formed their new government.

As the house neared completion, Filippo planned to return to Williamsburg because his frigate was nearing arrival with his shipments of goods from Italy and in order to fetch Mrs. Martin and Maria from Eppes's home and help settle them into Colle. Since Adams passed through Monticello on his way to do more business in Williamsburg, the two men rode together, making plans all the way for Filippo's shipments but also talking of government ideas. Surprisingly, Adams failed to mention one thing until the night before their arrival in Williamsburg: that the other business Adams planned to complete in Williamsburg was marriage.

Filippo congratulated his friend, but Adams, rather than discuss his own soon-to-be-bride, used the last day of their drive to advise Filippo to marry Mrs. Martin before he moved her and her daughter to Colle.

"I support them in honor of my friendship with her husband," Filippo reminded Adams. "While I vowed my financial support, I don't think I need also forfeit my liberty."

"You need a woman about the house with an attachment to you. With a reason to commit to the care of the home, and its master."

"Mrs. Martin has a bit too much vanity for my liking. How much more will that blossom if she is no longer indebted to me?"

"Then do it for Maria, who needs to make a good match so you won't have to support her for the rest of her life," Adams suggested. "If you all continue to live together without the benefit of marriage, Maria will never be able to find a husband. London is much more sophisticated, but in this country, the least suspicion of illicit behavior will ruin her—and you, for the man will always be assumed to be the seducer."

For Maria's sake, Filippo took Adams's advice and married Mrs. Martin the day after their arrival in Williamsburg. The ceremony took place in the home of justice of the peace Richard Randolph II. The day after that, the new couple called on Lord Dunmore, royal governor of the Virginia colony, to complete Filippo's application to become a naturalized citizen of his chosen new home. Conscious of his new role as husband, Filippo disliked the way the governor treated his own wife in front of guests, and feared for how he treated her when they were alone. He thought of his sister and mother, still living under the tyranny of Jacopo, and it reminded Filippo that liberty ought to be extended to all people.

At dinner, Lord Dunmore disturbed Filippo all the more by imagining that as a newcomer and a recent resident of London, Filippo sided with Britain. As the governor liked the sound of his own voice so well, Filippo found no clear openings in conversation, but this proved to be a useful way to learn more about what the governor had in store for the colonists. At that time, the British strategy to keep the colonists in line consisted of divide et impera, or attacking each colony separately, hoping to keep them all disconnected as no one colony could ever hope to fight England on its own. To counter this strategy, the Virginia Assembly had elected a Committee of Seven whose job involved corresponding with leaders of all the other colonies and transmitting word of any new attacks immediately to all the other colonies. Lord Dunmore dismissed the power of such a group outright, but his superiors back in London thought that move too weak and wanted the committee dissolved immediately.

Filippo left Lord Dunmore's home the next morning with the governor none the wiser as to his own burgeoning feelings for the revolutionaries. While he returned to live at Colle, he found himself spending more and more time at Monticello as he and Jefferson decided to collaborate on the writing of a periodical that would show people the necessity of preparing themselves in case of attack by the Regulars on order from the crown.

As they each played devil's advocate in a debate over taking such a strong step toward the independence of the colonies, Filippo warned Jefferson, "If we do this, there will be no turning back."

"I don't believe I want to turn back anymore," Jefferson responded.

With that, the two men began spending intense hours bent over their quill pens writing their original essays and then editing each other's work. Filippo wrote in Italian and Jefferson translated his words into English. The exercise deepened each man's understanding of the nuances of the other's language, which made the work even more enjoyable, despite the danger of their action.

"How clear is this?" Jefferson asked as he glanced back at his paper. "American lands are made subject to the demands of British creditors, while their own lands were still continued unanswerable for their debts; from which one of these conclusions must necessarily follow, either that justice is not the same in America as in Britain, or else…"

"Or else," Filippo composed out loud, "or else that the British parliament pay less regard to it here than there."

"*Sì, grazie,*" said Jefferson.

"Keep this up and we'll make a proper Italian of you."

"Right now I'm more focused on making proper Americans of us all. Without getting executed in the process."

To that end, the men decided it was not yet safe to attach their names to these inflammatory essays as they could be used as evidence of treason against the king.

"We each have wives to consider in this risk," Jefferson said.

Because he could not settle on the proper pseudonym for himself, Jefferson signed his articles "from a correspondent in Virginia." Filippo had no trouble deciding on another name, and so he became "Furioso."

The first fruits of their joint intellectual labor appeared in 1774 in the *Virginia Gazette.* Authored by Furioso and published in Italian, it read: "*Tutti gli uomini sono per natura egualmente liberi e indipendenti. Quest' eguaglianza e' neccessaria per costituire un governo libero. Bisogna che ognuno sia uguale all'oltro nel diritto natural."*

Beneath that section, Jefferson's translation appeared: "All men are by nature equally free and independent. This equality is necessary in order to create a free government. All men must be equal to each other in natural rights."

Soon Jefferson encouraged Filippo to write his thoughts out in English and Jefferson would make any small grammatical changes necessary. "You have a way of expressing yourself in which I cannot translate without weakening the effect. Your phraseology is not pure English, but everyone will understand you and the effect will be more forceful. That is what matters," Jefferson said.

The next essay appeared out of this new way of collaborating and, true to Jefferson's prediction, caused a stir.

"The British government has never been free at the peak of its perfection and our own was nothing more than a bad copy of it.... They are four hundred years behind the times so the time has come to change ways."

As the men read their handiwork over brandy that night at Monticello, they knew there was no going back now.

Chapter Ten

ELECTED TO REPRESENT HIS NEW COUNTRY

Most locals understood Furioso to be Filippo, right down to the fact that each name had seven letters and began with "F" and ended with "O," and most agreed with his writings. Filippo and Jefferson kept publishing essays about the issues of the day, including the need for religious tolerance and support for women's interests, and finally Filippo found a way to address an issue that had bothered him from the beginning: the abolition of slavery.

His views currently were on the side of the gradual abolition that was being advocated in many northern colonies. As Americans rallied for their own freedom, some had begun to see the hypocrisy evident in holding others in bondage. John Adams had written to them about a petition in Massachusetts from an enslaved man named Felix who asked for freedom for all with eloquent words Adams sent them: "We have no Property. We have no Wives. No Children. We have no City. No Country. But we have a Father in Heaven." According to Adams, it had opened the floodgates for petitions from others in other colonies.

Benjamin Franklin's letters were filled with plans for an actual Abolitionist Society, but being Franklin, he was collecting members and financial support before settling on a name. He wrote asking Filippo and Jefferson if they preferred Society for the Relief of Free Negroes Unlawfully Held in Bondage or the simpler Pennsylvania Abolition Society. Filippo liked the former because of its emotional appeal, but Jefferson balked at the use of the word "Unlawfully" as slavery had been a legal form of labor all his life.

Filippo found it hard to know he and Jefferson were in disagreement about this topic. So far, Filippo operated Colle on paid labor, or what was being called Free Labor in that the laborers were free to keep the fruits of their labor. When he needed to use extra workers, he hired enslaved men from Monticello with the understanding from Jefferson that he would pay those men directly and they would keep their wages. Traditionally, slave owners hired men out and kept the wages for themselves, but for his friend, Jefferson conceded this new way of doing business.

Even though some in the South were calling for gradual abolition, arguments for slavery still rang the loudest at the local taverns and dinner tables. Some used ancient philosophers to advocate for slavery, with Aristotle being a favorite thanks to his opinion that "From the hour of their birth, some men are marked out for subjection, others for rule." One argument centered on the idea that slavery existed in the Bible, so therefore it followed that God approved of it and to go against slavery was to go against God. Another belief focused on the idea that slaves were not fully human. Here Filippo countered with the words of the recently published poet Phillis Wheatley, the first literary work published by an enslaved person. He quoted her "On Being Brought from Africa to America" in one of his essays on the subject:

'Twas mercy brought me from my Pagan land,
Taught my benighted soul to understand
That there's a God, that there's a Saviour too:
Once I redemption neither sought nor knew.
Some view our sable race with scornful eye,
"Their colour is a diabolic die."
Remember, Christians, Negros, black as Cain,
May be refin'd, and join th' angelic train.

In his essay Furioso insisted that any being who could understand form, rhythm, language, and emotion so well as to create that poem could be nothing other than fully human.

"Yes, I see the evidence of her humanity," Jefferson said during their initial discussion over the essay and its contents. "But we have no sure proof that she was not aided in this work by her master or mistress in order to create a sort of phenomena that would bring them further profit."

"Who has sure proof that either of us writes what we say we write?" Filippo said. "Many will say I cannot know the language well enough to express myself within it without aid…."

"It is not slavery that is so bad as the slave trade," Jefferson countered, sticking to the subject. "The slave trade is an execrable commerce, an assemblage of horrors, cruel war against human nature itself, violating its most sacred rights of life and liberties."

"I believe that to be true of slavery as well," said Filippo gently. "Not merely of the trade."

On this night George Washington had come to dinner on his way to Lynchburg on business and contributed to the debate. "Slavery has made human beings into money," he said unhappily.

"Like cattle in the market, this disgusts me. I intend on my death for all my slaves to be freed."

Filippo could not hold back the truth. "But that depends on if your Martha precedes you in death, does it not? For as I understand it, many of those slaves came to you in marriage as dower slaves."

"That is true of many men I know," admitted Washington, "including my host, who gained many of his workforce from his own Martha, am I correct?"

Watching the two men squirm a bit at these truths made Filippo once again pleased with his experiment in indentured service. He still believed that men who had something to gain at the end of their service, and could see the end of their service in sight, worked harder to earn those rewards.

Despite their differing opinions on certain controversial topics—or because of the deft way Filippo managed to mention those topics and stir discussion without creating dissent—and thanks to his growing friendships with other men of means, Filippo was elected as a representative by a convention of like-minded colonists interested in breaking from England. They had to call their group a convention rather than an assembly because only the governor could call an assembly, and he was meticulously appointing only those men he thought maintained complete loyalty to London. The Virginia convention met anyway, and when they elected a Committee of Twelve to maintain order and communicate with other colonies, Filippo garnered more votes than most other nominees. Jefferson could not be on the committee as he was a member of the convention that created it. The committee then chose Filippo to be one of two administrators to handle the care of the local poor in their parish.

In the midst of all this politicking, both Jefferson and Filippo still carried the responsibility of managing their agricultural interests and, like all farmers, dealing with the weather. In his continued love of the Italian language, Jefferson recorded in his garden book the planting not of apricots and cherries, but of *albicocche* and *ciliegi*. Filippo had given his friend apricot stones and almost two hundred cherry pits. Jefferson named his trees Cornelian cherry trees, and cultivated them for fresh and preserved fruits. Filippo continued the cultivation of wine—and almonds, olives, and more—but the most successful of all became a Mediterranean form of corn, a fifty-day maize that the neighborhood nicknamed "Mazzei's corn" because he had introduced it and it grew so well. In this first harvest, Filippo's men identified thirty-six varieties of wild grapes on the estate from which they made wine; Filippo shared the bottles with dinner guests and his men were free to sell the excess for personal profit. Almonds were also thriving at both Colle and Monticello that year.

All went well until the spring of 1774—May 4, to be exact—when a frost fell, caused by a northwest wind, and ruined all the corn and wheat shoots that were just above ground. Bunches of grapes not yet harvested froze on the vine. Luckily, new shoots soon grew, but the output would not be what Filippo had calculated based on planting.

Working for the citizens and working on the land both involved travel to and from Williamsburg for Committee of Twelve meetings or to meet the ship Filippo owned that moved goods between that port and Livorno. On one trip, Filippo found himself in a debate with the treasurer of the colony, Nicholas Carter, who felt deeply that in all the action of revolution, "We may lose this Constitution."

Filippo had heard this argument before and quickly quashed it. "Had I such a constitution, I would think myself in consumption."

His remark made other men at the meeting laugh, and many agreed that the big "C" constitution of England was on its deathbed as any person suffering from consumption—which had the effect of turning more men toward their cause.

Between meetings Filippo dealt with business in the form of shipments from Livorno, which arrived at Williamsburg somewhat regularly. From one he collected two draft horses and six new young laborers to work at Colle. Antonio Giannini had been writing letters back home, and his vivid descriptions of the land and the life had drawn these men to sign up to work for Filippo. Most had hopes of earning their own farms someday, as all of them, like Filippo, were not firstborn sons and therefore not likely to inherit anything from their fathers in Italy.

The other new arrivals from this voyage were his friends Carlo and Gaspara Bellini. Carlo, a teacher, had traveled across Europe teaching modern languages, but returned to Florence, where he worked in the tax office of the Grand Duke of Tuscany. Being indifferent to religion, he had publicly disagreed with local clergy on several matters of doctrine, which barred him from a teaching position there. Filippo's letters, too, had attracted Carlo to Virginia.

"Welcome to America!" Filippo exclaimed upon meeting Carlo and Gaspara at the home of Colonel Cary, another friend Filippo had met through Thomas Adams. Cary had kindly offered the Bellinis his home as the boat had arrived a day earlier than Filippo had.

"It is good to be among free-thinking men again," said Carlo as they embraced in the European manner.

Cary, who was not yet used to such intimacy between male friends, merely proffered his hand to Filippo. Filippo accepted it, not wanting to cause his host any awkwardness, but was inwardly surprised at the intense protection of masculinity American men practiced.

"Free-thinking?" questioned Cary. "And he has not even met Mr. Jefferson yet."

"I can only imagine the conversations yet to be born around that magnificent table," Filippo said.

Filippo's prediction proved true. He and the Bellinis left the next morning and were dining at Monticello that evening. With Mrs. Martin having come down from Colle to entertain Gaspara, the men were free to discuss and debate philosophy, religion, and politics for hours over cigars and hot chocolate.

Jefferson's chocolate pot was tall and thin. When Bellini recognized it as being an import from Spain, Jefferson was so taken that he immediately sent off several letters to local friends advising them to hire the newly arrived linguistics specialist to tutor their sons as they approached admission to William and Mary—or Harvard. Two days later, the Bellinis moved into Colle with Filippo and his wife—whom most still referred to as "Mrs. Martin"—and Maria.

At the same time, convention members from across the colonies sent invitations to each other to attend one large congress designed to act in common cause against the crown. They wanted to meet in a central place and so chose Philadelphia for what would be called the Continental Congress. It convened there on September 5, 1774, and met for two solid months. Filippo helped elect his new friends Washington, Patrick Henry, Benjamin Harrison, and Richard Bland to the Virginia delegation and awaited news of their progress as he continued his correspondence work at home on the Committee of Twelve.

Through these letters exchanged with other committee men from around the colonies, Filippo learned about the boycott of British tea called for by Congress, and the Annapolis Tea Party that followed on October 19. Patriots burned the Maryland cargo ship HMS *Peggy Stewart* in Annapolis in retaliation for breaking the boycott. The ship's owner, Thomas Stewart, had hoped to bypass the boycott as tea still brought a fair price, and lied to customs about the content of seventeen packages aboard the boat, which also carried fifty-three indentured servants bound for the colonies. When the captain of the ship refused to lie to customs officials, Stewart's trick was discovered and an angry mob approached the docks.

"Listen to this," Filippo said to Jefferson the night he received this new correspondence. "An anonymous letter claims that 'the minds of the people were so inflamed that they threatened death to Mr. Stewart, and desolation to his store and dwelling-house.'"

"So what's to be done about it?" mused Jefferson, already considering three or four legal forms of retaliation.

"It's been done," said Filippo, reading from the letter. "The brig was moved away from other vessels with her sails and colors flying, and, after reading out a statement of apology for their conduct, Stewart and the joint owners of the vessel—"

"Yes, yes, go ahead," urged Jefferson, but Filippo enjoyed the theatrics of reading aloud enough to stretch out the tension, in an echo of his beloved author, Dante.

"The joint owners of the vessel set the vessel—and the tea— alight," Filippo continued. "Within a few hours, in the presence of a great number of spectators, the *Peggy Stewart* had burned down to the waterline. But first," he hastily added, "they removed all fifty-three of the indentured servants and all the crew, therefore harming no one."

"If only all war could be that clean," Jefferson thought aloud.

"And carefully calculated," added Filippo. "And safe."

The sober reality of their endeavors fell upon their shoulders simultaneously in that moment, becoming both a burden and a connection each man carried separately for the rest of his life.

The men continued meeting weekly to go over correspondence and were saddened to learn that as the men of Congress continued debating, it was becoming clear that far too many members of other delegations focused on remaining united to the country of their forefathers. Their major goal became writing a petition to King George III to rescind the Intolerable Acts, created by the king as punishment for the Boston Tea Party. As the body disbanded, they called for another Continental Congress in the event that their petition was unsuccessful, a fact that infuriated Filippo and Jefferson when they read about it in correspondence from John Adams, who was also angered by the weakness of the Congress.

Other Virginians displeased by these events decided to form the Independent Company of Albemarle County, a militia group that eventually included Filippo; Bellini, who joined to show his loyalty to his new country; and James Monroe, who had become a frequent guest at both Monticello and Colle between semesters at William and Mary. They all enlisted as volunteers in this militia convened by the Committee of Twelve rather than the royally approved assembly. All the writing Filippo and Jefferson had been doing had roused some of the locals into wanting to effect independence via the sword rather than the pen preferred by the two writers.

"But still you joined," Jefferson said to Filippo at one of their dinners. "I understand the young firebrands the militia attracts…but *you*? You joined."

"Yes," said Filippo thoughtfully. "I joined because I love my country and I love my countrymen. So many of them have come to ask advice of me, from over a week's ride away, because I have lived in England and they have not. If I am to advise them to rebel, and they want to contribute, but they haven't the skills to write essays or to attend Congress…if all they can do is defend their land, then that's what I advise."

"And if you don't take your own advice—"

"How can I expect *them* to take it?"

"Remind me not to debate you before the dessert course ever again," said Jefferson, who joined the Independent Company himself the next day.

Having no previous military experience, Filippo, Jefferson, and Bellini served as privates while one of Jefferson's workers—his overseer, in fact, having served in the French and Indian Wars—attained the rank of sergeant. The soldiers had asked Jefferson and Filippo to serve as officers. As a member of the convention Jefferson bowed to being too busy for leadership positions in more than one group, and Filippo deferred on the grounds of having no prior experience.

The sergeant clarified that they needed officers to advise as well as command, to which Filippo declared, "If the officers seek my opinion, I will gladly give it while in the guise of a mere private."

On March 23, 1775, the convention met again at St. John's Church in Richmond, Virginia, with Filippo, Jefferson, Washington, and Richard Henry Lee in attendance. All spoke passionately in favor of having a vote to approve a resolution forming more militias to defend against the crown, but the presence of the thirty-eight-year-old Patrick Henry stirred the most interest. As a member of the Continental Congress he had been decidedly angry by the lack of interest in independence. When Filippo had received a letter from Henry containing the text of his speech, he had sent on to other colonies the words that captured Filippo's own feelings best: "The distinctions between Virginians, Pennsylvanians, New Yorkers, and New Englanders are no more. I am not a Virginian; I am an American."

"It is not easy to say what we should have done without Patrick Henry," Jefferson said to Filippo over dinner at a local tavern. "He was before us all in maintaining the spirit of the Revolution."

"It is true we began as outliers, but I feel the momentum shifting to our cause," Filippo predicted. "Certain steps cannot be untaken. Did you see that unearthly fire burning in his eye? I now see it in many more faces I pass on the street."

After dinner they witnessed perhaps Henry's greatest hour. When called upon to speak in a room that still contained many declared loyalists to the king, Henry turned his attention to the British troops already mobilizing at ports across the colonies.

"Are fleets and armies necessary to a work of love and reconciliation?" he asked. "Have we shown ourselves so unwilling to be reconciled that force must be called in to win back our love?… Has Great Britain any enemy, in this quarter of the world, to call for all this accumulation of navies and armies? No, sir, she has none. They are meant for us; they can be meant for no other."

While others would write to their families and friends focusing on the ending lines of Henry's speech—"Give me liberty or give me death"—Filippo thought Henry's theatrics overdid the point and took away from its power. As he spoke those words the orator held his wrists together as though they were manacled and raised them toward the heavens, then he mimicked the breaking of the chains, grasped an ivory letter opener, and plunged the letter opener toward his heart. For years afterward, even when Filippo would come to write his own history of the Revolution, Henry's words that struck him deepest, the words that caught fire, were: "We have been spurned, with contempt, from the foot of the throne...we must fight! I repeat it, sir, we must fight! An appeal to arms and to the God of Hosts is all that is left us!"

Silence filled the room following Henry's conclusion. Then a loyalist member still in hope of reconciling with England stood and declared Henry's speech "infamously insolent" and demanded that the convention vote against the resolution to create more militias. Other loyalists began talking among themselves and Filippo sensed the tide swinging back to safety. Incensed, he jumped to his feet.

"Let no man deny what we have heard here," Filippo began. "If we do not wish to risk becoming its victim, we have to arm ourselves. The result will necessarily be either complete freedom or the harshest slavery."

As his words rang through the church, Jefferson stood, and then Richard Henry Lee, and all the other Patriots present, lending their support to the resolution, which passed by just a few votes—but it passed.

When Lee announced the votes, Filippo commented to those around him, "The sword is now drawn and God knows when it will be sheathed."

Chapter Eleven

FEET ON THE GROUND TO STAND THEIR GROUND

After the vote, the Virginia Convention placed Patrick Henry at the head of the militia, tasked with gathering enough men and arms to defend the colony. Men proved plentiful, but a more serious concern arose when the militias went in search of firearms to buy and found the English had cut off the supply of both firearms and ammunition, a trick they had played on the Native Americans in the many skirmishes between the two over the last century. The Patriots were forced to stock up with old shotguns and learn the art of mixing the gunpowder and manufacturing the musket balls that fit each man's individual rifle.

Filippo, responding to one of his many letters from another colony, was infuriated to find that the colonists were contemplating a war with only one gunpowder mill, the Frankford Mill in Pennsylvania.

"It cannot be expected to keep up with the demand, much less be kept in the supplies needed to make gunpowder," he said to Bellini one day at dinner.

"My specialty is languages, not chemistry," the teacher said, so Filippo described the ingredients of gunpowder—sulfur, charcoal, and nitre, also known as saltpeter—and the process of procuring all these ingredients. He proudly explained how a trade in native sulfur was already in place with Sicily, so only the amounts had to be increased, and charcoal and saltpeter could be obtained locally. Since natural saltpeter was a leachate of manure, the contents of barnyards, outhouses, and bat-cave deposits were considered the property of the government. To maximize production, women were called into service to supervise the production of homemade saltpeter. The process involved soaking soil in urine from both animals and humans, allowing it to dry, then boiling it to produce saltpeter—a job the women disliked immensely. Filippo and Bellini could not bring themselves to describe the process to their wives, leaving that up to Martha Jefferson, who had learned the process in a letter from Abigail Adams.

Meanwhile, their neighborhood had another issue to manage. On March 27, 1775, Jefferson's further involvement with the militia came into question as the Virginia Convention elected him to represent them at the Second Continental Congress. He and Filippo debated his joining that body as they rode across Colle one morning checking the grape harvest.

"Everything we have done to this point, from our essays to the colonial convention, could be credited to our being good subjects to a bad king," Filippo offered. "But with the assembly calling the convention treasonous, and with you joining under your real name…"

"Yes, I've been thinking along those lines as well," Jefferson concluded. "My family and my lands are at risk."

"As is your life."

"If that's the case, then there's no reason to worry about militia skirmishes, now is there? I could be just as wounded sitting in this congress. Spies will be everywhere, eager to inform the Regulars."

"But you're going to go anyway, aren't you?"

"Franklin will be there. Again." Jefferson replied. "And Adams. John—not Thomas, of course. And Samuel."

"I wish I were on that list," Filippo said.

"We'll need men back in the colonies, in the militias, to back up whatever we do. And I'll need a friend on site helping Martha manage, until I return...*if* I return."

"*When* you return. When you return, all will be in order. I'll save the finest sampling of this year's wine to share at your table on the night of your return."

"I'd bring some with me. I'd be all right around Franklin as he prefers beer, but heaven knows Adams would drink me under any table."

"Thomas or Samuel?"

"John. His Abigail wrote my Martha that the man takes three to four glasses of Madeira before bed."

"We have been known to imbibe three or four at dinner," Filippo reminded him, happy to be taking his mind off the dangerous turn their lives were taking.

"At dinner," Jefferson emphasized. "When wine is meant to be taken. My physician insists anything later in the evening does not sit well in a man's stomach."

"Perhaps the sour stomach explains Adams's famous attitude," Filippo said in jest.

Before Jefferson could leave for Philadelphia, he joined Filippo, James Monroe, Bellini, a young Italian laborer from Colle named Vincenzo, and the rest of the one-hundred-man militia as they marched on Williamsburg under the command of Patrick Henry. Two incidents converged to call these men to action in April of

1775. In the first, word came that Lord Dunmore feared losing control of the colony to the Patriots, so he instead gave control of the Williamsburg arsenal to Lieutenant Henry Colins and ordered him to transport nearly fifteen half-barrels of powder down the Quarterpath Road to the James River and onto the HMS *Magdalen,* where Colins served as captain. In the second incident, Patriots in Hampton reported sighting some English ships on the way, and spies in the area claimed they were troops sent to calm the Virginians. So the men of Colle and Monticello were on the march to meet them with whatever meager weapons they had been able to muster.

Along the way Filippo's company connected up with several other companies of men all headed toward the Governor's Palace for a confrontation. Among these new men came several of the Madison brothers, including James, who had been studying at the University of New Jersey but returned home to Montpelier, Virginia, as the conflict neared. As they prepared their blankets to sleep in the woods that first night, Filippo and Madison tried in vain to convince Monroe to turn back as he was by far the youngest of them all at the age of sixteen.

"Your parents will need someone to manage affairs at home," insisted Filippo.

"I have several brothers," Monroe replied. "Two of them already manage the plantation, which is why I could be spared to spend time at college."

"And in politics," Filippo noted. "John Adams wrote me something quite philosophical last month: 'We must study politics and war, that our sons may study mathematics and philosophy so their children may study painting, poetry, and music.'"

"He's defining this new race we call Americans," said Madison.

"He's defining me," said Monroe.

"Why waste all that potential?" asked Filippo, turning the conversation back to convincing Monroe to leave the front.

"I am young, yes, but so is this movement," Monroe stated. "I am here at the birth of this new country that will be my peer. I need to help it to its feet."

The next morning, happy news spread through the camp, courtesy of a contingent of men from Warwick, Virginia. They met privately with Patrick Henry, who then announced with yet more fanfare that when word of the Virginia men on the march reached the ships, the captains thought it best to embark again and avoid confrontation. A huge "Hurrah!" came from the men as Henry continued his speech. Filippo felt particularly proud when Henry singled out the support and loyalty of the Tuscans in their midst. Vincenzo, who was still learning English, had to ask Filippo to translate, which he did gladly.

"Only in this new land could a peasant draw the thanks of a lord," Vincenzo said in awe.

"Well, Mr. Henry is far from a lord," Filippo clarified. "And you are far from a peasant. That's not what's wanted here. Judging by the look on your face, I imagine you wouldn't exchange places with any lord right now."

After more backslapping all around, some men turned back for home, more interested in keeping the British away than antagonizing the governor. The men of Filippo's company continued toward Williamsburg and the Governor's Palace, hearing that Lord Dunmore now had his front door guarded with a contingent of gunmen who would fire if anyone broke down the door. He and his family evacuated to a ship in the harbor to avoid any harm. From there, he issued a proclamation against "a certain Patrick Henry and a Number of deluded Followers" who had organized "an Independent Company…

and put themselves in a Posture of War." Meant to scare the men away, the proclamation only angered them more and drew them around their new leader with ever more fervent loyalty. Together they attacked the palace and successfully seized the arsenal for future use by their militia.

Soon after, Jefferson left for the Second Continental Congress, which convened on May 10. Filippo took over the management of Monticello at a hazardous time. Dunmore had begun ordering raiding parties to attack the plantations of Virginia Patriots along the Potomac River. This put George Washington's Mount Vernon in particular peril as he was well known among those advocating for a break with England and his home sat right on the Potomac. In a letter to Filippo, congratulating him on the success of the militia and how it put Dunmore out to sea but still allowed him to menace them all, Washington noted there was still much work ahead: *"I do not think that forcing his lordship on shipboard is sufficient. Nothing less than depriving him of life or liberty will secure peace to Virginia, as motives of resentment actuate his conduct to a degree equal to the total destruction of that colony."*

The final straw that turned Virginians from the governor came when he issued Dunmore's Proclamation, offering freedom to any slave who fought for the Crown against the Patriots in Virginia. While Filippo agreed with the sentiment, turning their laborers against them at this crucial time caused even more of a threat than the arrival of the British troops.

By this point, Washington had joined Jefferson in Philadelphia, and on June 14, Congress voted to create a Continental Army and appoint Washington its commanding general. When Jefferson wrote him the news, Filippo quickly sent missives to all his other contacts in the colonies, urging them to prepare for war as he and the Madison brothers continued drilling with the militia. Things moved so swiftly and so much needed to be done that there was not enough time to handle it all. Daytime found Filippo managing both Colle and Monticello and attending militia meetings. Nights found him bent over his desk, quill in hand, reading and responding to letters from other committee men all around the colonies, from friends at the Continental Congress reporting on the debates to quartermasters from the front begging for supplies of food and ammunition. James Madison, with whom Filippo drilled in the militia company, had become a frequent visitor at Colle, often staying for dinner to collect more of the latest information and to help Filippo debate these ideas and the proper responses.

In the absence of Jefferson, many uneducated local men, small farmers, laborers, shopkeepers, and the like came to Filippo for advice on business or politics. He humbly thanked them for their compliments and learned that even if Jefferson had been in residence, Filippo's international experience was what drew them to see him. Having this moment of influence, Filippo could not help using it for purposes above and beyond urging these men to support the fight for political freedom.

"Now is the time to talk honestly about the emancipation of the slave," he began many of his meetings, both large and small. "Gradual manumission has become the way of the northern colonies and must surely follow here, once those in need of freedom are given the tools to make good use of that freedom."

Usually, smaller farmers, those who never had the funds to rely largely on enslaved labor, were amenable to the idea. It was among Filippo's closer friends, the larger planters, that the idea still spelled anathema. But the more he had a chance to bring up abolition, the more he did. Even Madison began to talk of the right time to free slaves.

"I never knew a planter to survive without slave labor," Madison admitted one night, "until I met you."

"I will admit in all fairness that vineyards and fruit trees require less manual labor than tobacco or wheat production," began Filippo. "But even should I have chosen those products— and I do grow maize and quite a few things on this land—I would have found ways to pay my workers. Indentured servants work harder for a reward both financial and personal. What does the slave earn for their labor? Nothing but hell."

"I agree in many ways," said Monroe, who had come by that night to help with the correspondence. "But my own father reminds me often that slavery is in the Bible and so…"

"I have heard this argument often myself," Filippo said. "But who is the hero of the Old Testament?"

"Moses, I should say," responded Monroe thoughtfully.

"And Moses freed the slaves," said Filippo gently. "So to me, that means God disapproves of slavery—in all forms."

These conversations continued with many local men over the next few months. Now that everyone knew the man named Furioso who wrote essays for the local *Virginia Gazette* was indeed Filippo, there was a call for him to present his ideas as speeches at local churches. His particular focus at such events was the religious freedom he and Jefferson had discussed over many a dinner. On one such Sunday, Filippo could sense the crowd swaying to his side as he took a page out of Patrick Henry's performance and thundered, "We will be the first country to demonstrate both the justice of religious freedom and the benefits derived from it—especially the removal of all jealousies!" After such moments, many congregants told Filippo he ought to have considered a life in the church. Instead, he felt he had taken a life in the military, between drilling with the militia and traveling locally with recruitment officers to gather soldiers for Washington's Continental Army. To encourage possible recruits after the army's failure at the Battle of Bunker Hill, Filippo reminded them that the number of British losses, among men and arms, showed that the Continental Army could succeed as long as it continued to add new, fresh troops to its rolls and keep up the production of ammunition.

In early May, a delegation of Presbyterians came to Colle to ask Filippo to stand for election to the Fifth Virginia Convention in Williamsburg. Though they knew him to be a Catholic and a member of the vestry of St. Anne's Parish, they also knew his writings on the need for religious freedom for all, and they wanted such a man who would fight for this shared cause. He was already hosting a visit by John Henderson and Edmund Pendleton regarding the upcoming Virginia Convention.

In his natural humility, Filippo begged off, saying, "There is no lack in the county of people more capable than I."

"Your modesty becomes a man of your station," Henderson said. "After Thomas Jefferson, you are the best leader in the county. You are educated and many are not. You have lived in England and know the English mind, and we do not."

"Of course, that very fact might keep you from winning the first election," noted Pendleton. "Some who do not know you as *we* know you may believe your sentiments still lie with the king."

"As is true of many of our brethren," Filippo said, "but not of me."

He could sense Pendleton's participation in this set of neighbors came more from a need to be involved in all aspects of this new order than from any deep reverence for Filippo and his philosophies. Consequently, Filippo knew he would have to keep an eye on this gentleman.

"Are there any other unfavorable points about me that might hinder our work together?" he asked.

Henderson shook his head, but as Filippo suspected, Pendleton continued. "Well, sir, there is the question of where you stand on this issue of equality...."

"You have heard me speak of abolition," Filippo began.

"I meant...of religion," finished Pendleton. "Are you not, in fact, a Catholic, with men among your own family who have taken up the collar?"

Filippo cut him off politely, waving away Pendleton's point. "Yes, there are those who will accuse me of popery, but if you read my words, you will know that I don't believe any government can police the hearts or minds of men. My time in England showed me the foolishness of Henry VIII and how his want of a divorce destroyed the peace of a nation for many generations to come. Therefore, religious freedom is the only possible solution."

Pendleton had no response to such a passionate, well-informed stance, and so he and Henderson left with the agreement that Filippo would allow his name to be put up for election. But in the end, Filippo thought better of it.

"But why?" asked Madison, who had agreed to place himself on the ballot. "Did you let all that talk of popery affect you?"

"No," responded Filippo slowly and thoughtfully. "No. I believe I know the English language...well enough to be able to write it fairly readily...for in writing one has time to think. But...to be able to address a popular assembly, one must have the proper words—and phrases—on the tip of one's tongue, for these are frequently more effective than sound, logical reasoning."

Filippo also conceded that he was more useful in writing and publishing on timely topics and in private conversations with high-ranking men, so he began that work in earnest. He spent his nights entertaining dinner debates with landowners from around the colony and his spare time writing to members of Congress. Instead of the Virginia Convention, he took a position with the County Committee of Safety, which governed Albemarle during the Revolution and allowed him to stay close to home and his obligations to both Colle and Monticello.

One of Filippo's next pamphlets that Jefferson gladly had copied and dispensed to all members was his "Instructions of the Freeholders of Albemarle County to Their Delegates in Convention." One of the key points Filippo made in the document covered the need to discontinue the mandatory contributions local governments had been making to ministers, because they were only paid out to clergy in the established Anglican Church. In a few months' time, cities all around the colony suspended those ministerial taxes, and after the Revolution, naturally, they never returned. In the pamphlet, Filippo also argued that the colonies should have "but one and the same constitution."

Filippo sent letters to friends in the Second Continental Congress and the Fifth Virginia Convention advocating independence, and the Virginia Convention declared it first.

"Now the real work of government begins," he wrote in a letter to Jefferson. *"Putting down on paper what we stand for and how we will maintain those ideals—whilst surrounded by other men not quite as committed to those ideals."*

Jefferson reported similar clashes taking place in the Second Continental Congress, where he, Franklin, and John Adams were among the loudest in the call for independence. Wanting Virginia to be represented strongly in whatever decisions were to be made, Jefferson asked Filippo to send him copies of the various documents being prepared by the local convention. Filippo sent the Virginia Declaration of Rights and the early drafts of what would become their first constitution. He also signed a petition for Jefferson's Committee on Religion to abolish spiritual tyranny. Some delegates worried that such mail would be intercepted by the British, traveling as it did so haphazardly from men who happened to be doing business between Williamsburg and Philadelphia, but most missives seemed to reach their intended audience. Filippo concluded that none had fallen into the hands of the British by the fact that he himself had not yet been arrested. It appeared British interest lay in messages Washington sent back and forth from the battlefields to Congress.

"Our mother country has no belief that what they call this little insurrection will succeed," Filippo said to Madison, who had been elected to the convention but was home at Montpelier for a week to help out while his father had been taken ill. "So all they care for now is word that will help them crush our army. Our future plans are of no interest to them."

"That's to their detriment," Madison declared over their third glass of wine with dinner. "For I foresee…"

"What?" Filippo asked. "What exactly do you see?"

"Free men running their affairs as they see fit."

"If only we could get this turgid body of delegates to agree how that can be!" said Filippo with a smile.

Filippo soon learned, according to letters from Jefferson, Adams, and Franklin, that a similar question had arisen at Congress. The three men had been tasked with creating a document that could explain to the powers of Europe why this rebellion was a fair response to unjust governance, with Jefferson as the principal writer. Jefferson further wrote of how he wished to be back in the library at Monticello for this project, arguing with Filippo over each word and phrase, but since circumstances made that impossible, they would have to resign themselves to frequent letters. Filippo sent Jefferson the Virginia Declaration of Rights and Jefferson sent back drafts of his Declaration of Independence, pointing out the places where he had incorporated several of the points Filippo had argued so strongly for in the Virginia version. Filippo sent back his ideas as if the two men were once again across the table at Monticello—something they knew would rarely happen again in the tumultuous new world they were helping to create, if they both survived the creation.

Chapter Twelve

DEFENDING VIRGINIA WITH ALL THEY HAD TO OFFER

As the Americans began to gain victories, or at least kept fighting despite defeats, the Royal Governor Lord Dunmore gave orders to burn the waterfront buildings in Norfolk, Virginia, from which Patriot troops had been firing on his ships. On New Year's Day in 1776, the fire spread, burning much of the city with the help of over four thousand British troops who had disembarked to raid the town of any supplies useful to the Patriots. Many of the shop owners still held loyalist ties to the king and they fled to the British ships in the harbor for protection. Most of the refugees sailed south and resettled in Florida, which was still under the dominion of Spain. Dunmore and his family retreated to New York, never to return to the palace or his duties, leaving Colonel Robert Howe of the Continental Army and a regiment of North Carolina soldiers in control of the town. At first Howe called for more troops to hold the town, but upon realizing that the British fleet could isolate them, he recommended to the Virginia Convention that the town be abandoned and rendered useless to their enemy.

Upon reading this news in a letter from Thomas Adams, who had been in Norfolk, Filippo went immediately to the new governor, his old friend Patrick Henry, to find out how soon the Albemarle militia could march to the area to help stabilize the situation.

Henry would not hear of it. "You know as well as I do that there are greater ways for men of our station to serve the country than in the bearing of arms," he insisted.

"You led the militia at the Governor's Palace," Filippo reminded him.

"And now I lead us all, civilians and soldiers," Henry said. "Your writing, your speaking out in public, this changes minds, and minds support the military."

This time Filippo did not agree with his friend. Disappointed, he went straight to General Washington for a commission, but by that time, Washington had received a letter for Filippo with instructions directly from the governor.

"How can he issue an order refusing me the right to leave the county?" Filippo demanded.

"We are a country at war," Washington said, too weary of the cost he had seen in loss of men and lack of support to fight one more fight.

"I refuse his order," Filippo declared.

"You are free to do that," Washington said. "But I am not." He presented a second order, addressed to Washington, forbidding him to recruit Filippo. "I take my orders from the legislature."

Filippo returned to the governor to complain, but by that time another crisis was at their doorstep. After a skirmish in a local swamp, forty wounded English soldiers were carried to the Williamsburg hospital by men of the Continental Army, who could not leave them to die. Filippo knew that his medical training, no matter how long it had been since he had practiced,

made his aid necessary. He worked two solid days helping stabilize the worst wounds, all the while hearing the stories of the
fight and realizing the bodies he worked on belonged to mere
boys, many of whom were not English at all, but German mer-
cenaries hired to fight. England wasn't sending their best soldiers
to the fight—they were sending their most expendable.

Filippo was both saddened at the waste of life and strangely
sure this was a sign the Patriots had a real chance to win, for
just as he believed enforced laborers never did their best work
without some hope for future reward, he knew soldiers would
not long stay loyal to a country that treated them as cannon
fodder. In fact, many of these English troops spoke highly of the
Continental Army men they met on the battlefield, especially
those who had waded into the swamps where many of them
lay immobilized. The Americans had carried their English enemies upon their shoulders until they reached drier land. Then
the American officers used their own wagons to transport those
men who could not walk to the local hospital.

"No," Filippo thought as he worked. "Men would not long
fight for a king they didn't know when they found the enemy so
much like them."

Filippo noticed other flaws in the British plan as well. To
bolster the king's subjects back in England, their newspapers
reported large numbers of Englishmen flooding into the Royal
Army to help put down the insurrection. Rather than instill terror
in the Americans, the news drew hundreds more volunteers from
all over the colonies, determined to help stand against the flood of
what to them were foreign invaders. Officers of the Continental
Army asked Filippo and other County Committee of Safety
members to send letters to colonial governors begging them to
keep the men at home, raising food and collecting other necessary

supplies for the army. To that end, Governor Henry asked Filippo to return to Colle and Monticello and be in charge of such things in that area.

En route home, Filippo stopped off at an inn in Richmond and there received the wonderful news of the American success at Fort Ticonderoga from locals hosting a celebration.

"Fifty-nine!" one man shouted as he downed the last drops of his tankard of beer.

Approaching the bar, Filippo said a hearty "Blessings on your birthday, friend."

The man slapped Filippo on the back and smiled, "Birthdays? What do you take me for? I'm forty-four if I'm a day."

Another man stepped up. "We're drinking to the fifty-nine cannons Washington captured over there at Fort Ticonderoga today!"

"On their way to defending those Puritan prigs in Boston, they are," the first man said.

Suddenly, everyone had an insult for Bostonians on their lips, but Filippo halted them.

"In this fight we are all Americans, are we not?" Filippo asked.

That settled the men a bit and one bought Filippo a beer. Sensing he was a man of education and deeper connection to the events at hand, they all sat down to share what news each man had and debate what it all meant. Filippo could see from this random set of stories that his prediction was coming true. Passion among lesser-trained men was beating ambivalence among the more highly trained army.

"And the British soldiers are harming the king's cause in a new way," he volunteered. "Merely by desertion."

"English soldiers deserting?" the barkeep asked incredulously.

"I have reliable word that many English soldiers, scheduled to be flogged for minor offences, ran off and switched sides—and the Continental Army certainly welcomes men with such training. I have that from Washington's own mouth." Filippo touched his pocket, indicating Washington's letter was there.

"I heard some that run away are even buying land," another man contributed.

"I have no definite word on that," Filippo admitted, "but it wouldn't surprise me. Land is what drew most of us here—and land is why we fight."

The barkeep liked how the discussion kept the men in the inn longer, which kept them ordering more beer. "I heard that Washington's got his hands full with what to do with those who won't desert on account of what the Regulars are doin' with our boys when they capture 'em," he added.

Filippo felt as if the young man had been reading his own correspondence as that's what Washington had been writing him about over the course of the last month. Normal procedures of war required prisoner exchanges after each battle—five privates for one sergeant, two sergeants for one colonel, etc. But the English refused at first to consider men of the Continental Army to be soldiers from another country since they did not recognize America as its own country. King George's latest proclamation declared the colonies to be in rebellion, and threatened to punish anyone found wielding arms against his government. So when the Regulars took prisoners, they treated them like criminals, as happened in the case of Colonel Ethan Allen, a case causing considerable anger judging by stories in the many colonial newspapers—and the ones being told at inns like this all across the colonies.

"Heard they put our man Ethan Allen in chains," the barkeep said. "Hands and feet."

"And him a colonel, too," the barkeep's wife added quietly as she cleared the table. "Disgraceful for a gentleman like that to be treated no better."

Thanks to his busy correspondence schedule, and being on his way back from seeing the governor in Williamsburg, Filippo could assure them that that situation was in hand.

"Just the other day General Washington sent a letter to General Howe demanding respectable treatment for our colonel or we'd do the same by their brigadier general, a man by the name of Prescott," said Filippo.

"Washington'd prefer tradin' 'em to having to keep 'em," declared the barkeep, who clearly relished being the most informed man in the room and didn't like the idea that Filippo bested him with the most current news.

"Heard he had to keep some of them, had to pay his own money to feed them," another man said.

"Never," said the barkeep. "Never is a man o' that standin' goin' to pay to feed a prisoner."

"As a matter of fact," Filippo said gently, "he is doing exactly that. If the king won't agree to trading, then we'll have to build camps. They're planning one in Pennsylvania and I proposed one of the camps be here in Virginia. In Winchester."

As the drunken men began arguing over the benefits and disadvantages of having prisoners in their midst, Filippo slipped upstairs to his room, hoping to avoid the inevitable clash before crockery was broken, perhaps over his head.

≈

For all his efforts to aid the fledgling United States, Filippo was asked to do one more thing: leave the new country he had come to love in order to secure support from foreign governments for the impending war against England. This support would include seeking loans, buying—or rather, smuggling—weapons to the colonies, and obtaining political and military information useful to the fledgling nation.

He had been at Colle for a short time, managing agricultural issues for both his land and Jefferson's, corresponding with other leaders of the Revolution, and continuing to write essays encouraging more of the Tories to see the reality of the new country and disavow their love of England. All this work involved frequent travel back and forth from Williamsburg, and during one trip a courier awaited him at his inn with an urgent letter from Jefferson. Jefferson asked that Filippo burn the letter in the fire after reading it, and that he not answer it in writing, but rather go to see Governor Henry the next day for a private audience between the two men to discuss a request.

"At this kind of meeting, during wartime, one does not want too much in writing," Henry said when his attendant left the room. "Spies are everywhere."

"On their side and on ours," Filippo said.

"You know what happened to Nathan Hale?"

"I'll never forgive them for hanging that poor soul," Filippo said sadly. "So young. Like so many of our soldiers...so much promise."

"They all have promise. We had promise when we were but lads and now look at us." He tried to smile, but Filippo sensed an inner tension and something he hadn't felt from Henry before: fear. "I've asked you here to make a formal request based on a letter you should have received from our mutual friend, Mr. Jefferson."

"I have read the letter," Filippo responded without hesitation. "I look forward to the additional details he promised you would provide."

Henry outlined a plan conceived by himself, Jefferson, and George Mason. The colonies needed more money and more supplies or the war would be lost. That assistance could only come from European countries, especially those who were also enemies of England, or were willing to risk becoming the enemies of England in order to attain the undying friendship of the Americans. Fostering those kinds of relationships required an agent who had a facility with language, a knowledge of how to move among the peoples of the world at all levels, the skill to manage large sums of money, and the ability to make large purchases of weapons and supplies and arrange their delivery across the ocean to the Continental Army.

"And such a strong love of this new land that he would risk his own life to offer this kind of support," Henry finished.

"In other words," said Filippo, "me."

"Will you do it?"

"Yes," Filippo said, once again without hesitation, though it would mean separation from the land and relationships he had painstakingly cultivated these past years. He, Jefferson, and the Reverend Charles Clay of the Calvinistical Reformed Church of Charlottesville, Virginia, had just started a new, independent church in the area. Now, Filippo would not have the chance to join his friends and neighbors in worship, but if it would help that land and those people for him to be far away for a while, then Filippo would heed the call.

Shortly thereafter, Madison, now serving as one of the governor's councilors, came into the meeting with all the papers required for Filippo's new job: his letter of commission to prove his mission was approved by the Continental Congress, letters of credit for up to one million English pounds, letters of introduction to friends and allies in Europe. Madison had also arranged a cover story for Filippo's trip, spreading the word through intercepted letters and by starting rumors at local inns that Filippo's holdings in Tuscany required his immediate presence.

"Good luck to you, my friend," Madison said as he handed the packet to Filippo. "I hope and pray our paths will cross again and that we and our families will make it through this fight together."

"Families?" Filippo teased his friend, trying to keep such a tense moment as light as possible. "I pray by the end of this revolution you, my friend, will have found a wife deserving of you—and that you will be deserving of her."

Filippo left once again for home to prepare his employees for managing both plantations minus their owners, and to prepare his family for traveling. No one felt Mrs. Martin and Maria would be safe with him being so far away, in case the British marched this far into Virginia. So they, too, would have to return to Europe, but not be told the reason why, so as not to place them in jeopardy. Filippo found dealing with the workers far easier than dealing with his wife.

With the workers, Filippo knew immediately that he would place Antonio Giannini, one of the first men who had signed up to come with him to the colonies, in charge of planting and harvesting operations at Colle. Giannini would cover both Colle and Monticello for a short period between Filippo's departure and Jefferson's return from Congress. As to Carlo Bellini, Filippo encouraged the Virginia Council of State to hire him, describing Bellini as "a faithful & capable person to Act as Secretary & Interpreter of the French & other foreign Languages." With Jefferson filing his second recommendation, and since the foreign correspondence of Virginia had increased, Bellini gained the position of Clerk of Foreign Correspondence at £200 a year.

The other question—who would rent the home at Colle while Filippo was away—caused him momentary confusion and a bit of embarrassment. Upon returning home, he found a German officer of the British army hoping to rent Colle for the duration of his existence as a prisoner of war. As the British royal family was of German lineage, the two countries had been quite friendly with each other for a few generations, and so many German men volunteered to fight in the colonies. Captured after the Battle of Saratoga, General Riedesel, like all officers, was expected to pay for his upkeep until he could be exchanged for an American general after another battle and many negotiations across the sea. Riedesel had the less typical need of also housing his wife, Frederika Charlotte, and three daughters who had traveled with him and been captured with him. Frederika was in the process of publishing the letters and journal entries she had made relating to the War of the American Revolution and the capture of the German troops at Saratoga. The three daughters were all near the age of Jefferson's daughters and would make great companions, and the prisoner-of-war camp Albemarle Barracks could not hold children, so Riedesel hoped to rent out Colle.

"I would be most honored to invite you into my home," Filippo said to Riedesel in French, as that was the one language both men spoke. "But I have had news by letter today that Mr. Jefferson, not knowing your needs, has rented my home to a contingent of four British officers who have also been taken prisoner recently."

Seeing the disappointment on Riedesel's face, Filippo offered the general his own room as an accommodation until the officer could find something more suitable. He also agreed to sell Riedesel rights to the vegetable gardens at Colle, the six hen coops that produced eggs prodigiously, both of the duck breeds he raised on the land, as well as the two types of turkeys. For the rest of his supplies and livestock, Filippo arranged an auction that took four days but netted him a solid profit, proving his eye for product was strong.

In speaking to Maria later in the day, Filippo found she had read Jefferson's letter and had realized why he so hastily offered up Colle for rent. "One of these officers is said to play the violin quite well, according to Mr. Jefferson's letter," she said.

"Of course," Filippo said. "That is why he wants this set of men as neighbors for the duration of the war."

"With Mr. Jefferson playing the violincello so well and this man to accompany him, I can almost hear the beautiful music that will fill our rooms."

Maria had said "our" with a catch in her throat and Filippo realized that the young woman had become deeply fond of her home at Colle and quite probably did not want to leave, though she had said nothing when he first informed them. He had been so busy with all his considerations about this new commission that he had forgotten how it might affect the women who made up his legal family. While he and Mrs. Martin had maintained the marriage as more of a business association that allowed them to live together without damaging Maria's reputation, the young lady herself had seen Filippo as a father figure, and Colle and the surrounding countryside as a home she had come to know quite well, along with all the other young people in the neighborhood. Now Filippo threatened to drag her away, back to a country she barely remembered, without having told them the real reasons why, for their own protection in case they were stopped while traveling.

Filippo had to face another family issue beyond dealing with Maria and her sadness regarding the move, one that proved thornier. Mrs. Martin did not want to leave Colle, and the reason had nothing to do with loving the land or loving Filippo. Their relationship had been built on pragmatism—he needed to live up to his obligation to her late husband and, in truth, he had come to love young Maria as the daughter he had never had. But his opinion of Mrs. Martin had never changed. In their home she acted like royalty, bossing servants around and expecting deference on all things.

As he tried to discuss this situation delicately with his local friends without bringing insult to his wife, as that would be seen as ungentlemanly, Filippo learned that Mrs. Martin had made many social enemies in Albemarle County. Bellini insisted that she return to Europe with Filippo and that she stay there in some comfortable situation while he returned to Colle after the war.

"She makes everyone miserable in her presence," Bellini confessed. "Ordering them about, acting the queen. But worse..." He hesitated, but Filippo gestured that his friend should continue. "She tells everyone—though we all know the favor you are doing her husband and child—she tells everyone that you are cold and unkind to her. But we see with our own eyes what you have done, and still do."

The conversation was harder with Jefferson. Filippo learned that Martha Jefferson detested Mrs. Martin for her high-handed ways, but tolerated her out of fondness for Filippo.

"Because you defend her," Jefferson explained, "because you love her, we tried to love her, but she makes such action impossible. In my own home, Martha tells me, Mrs. Martin insults her table and her dress, but slightly, in that mean-spirited way of complimenting when you mean to slight."

"We made it clear from the start that this marriage was not about love," Filippo explained. "In fact, I was against it, but Thomas Adams insisted that you Americans would not understand our previous arrangement. That living together without the benefit of marriage, though I have never claimed those intimate benefits from Mrs. Martin, would not be abided in Virginia."

"Don't even ask Adams about her," said Jefferson. "Once he saw through her, and gave us the insight to do so as well, she cut him in all the parlors in the county. The things she said about him my wife would not repeat to me, but it caused her great discomfort for she loves him like a brother."

"As do I," said Filippo. "I am deeply saddened if anything related to me caused any discomfort to such a great lady. I acted as though I loved her because any lack of kindness toward a wife would reflect badly on her child, and frankly on my whole household."

"I agree with Bellini," said Jefferson. "If there is no love in your marriage, she must return to Europe with you. And stay. You will have done her a great service to leave her to live her own life, but with your support. Maria, however, is beloved by all the women. She ought return with you, and once this awful war is over, we can turn to the business of making a marriage for her that will allow her to take her place among the great ladies of Albemarle."

Relieved to know that Mrs. Martin's behavior had not affected Maria's chances, Filippo resolved to take them both on this trip, settle Mrs. Martin somewhere of her liking, and return with Maria, if the young woman so chose. This decision made their last two nights in Virginia difficult. The three of them stayed with the Jeffersons as Riedesel had taken residence fully.

"He even bought out your planned new neighbors," said Filippo. "So those musical nights might be off the agenda."

"Perhaps Mr. Jefferson can teach him," said Maria with a smile. She sat between her mother and Mrs. Jefferson, providing a buffer as each now knew through their husbands what they truly thought of each other.

When the men retired to the library for their last in-person conversation for however long it would be, Jefferson noted over a bottle of the wine they had created together, "I don't believe Washington had as tense a meeting with Howe. I am glad that you are well done with Mrs. Martin. While I do not wish ill on anyone, I fervently hope someday you will enjoy the feelings I share with Martha."

As the Mazzei party was taking their leave the next morning, Filippo took pride in seeing how much Mrs. Jefferson, who had three children of her own, fussed over Maria's traveling clothes, as if she were a daughter. As they entered the carriage that would bring them to the ship that would take them across the ocean, Maria had tears in her eyes. While it filled Filippo with happiness to know she loved the home he'd made for her, he hoped the tears weren't an omen for the success of the voyage.

Chapter Thirteen

WARTIME TRAVELS AND TRAVAILS

A week later they found themselves on a dock on the Rappahannock River, watching one hundred barrels of tobacco being loaded into the hold of the ship *Johnston* that would take Filippo's party to Nantes, France. Sale of the tobacco would cover Filippo's living expenses in Europe, though to keep his cover as an agent of the United States government, the barrels were listed on the manifest as fruits of his own lands, being sold in Europe for his own profit. Then, at the last minute, the captain, Andrew Peyton, demanded Filippo provide additional funds up front for the two berths he had booked, as if he didn't trust Filippo to finish the trip. Filippo had inquired about the man's loyalties and was told that Peyton, a Scotsman, had no love for the English king. This demand for extra funds was unsettling, yet Filippo had to get to Europe soon and no other ships were leaving the port in the near future, as traveling in wartime had become quite dangerous.

A new member of the Mazzei party, Francesco del Maglio, was making the journey with them, serving as groom and steward to the animals Filippo planned to sell in Europe. The rest of Filippo's Italian peasants would have their salary taken care of by the combined efforts of Riedesel, Jefferson, and the Continental Congress for as long as Filippo stayed in Europe. The peasants had given him a package of letters to deliver to their relatives back in Italy, some written by their own hand and others dictated to and then written by Maria for men who did not yet know how to write. Filippo also carried his own memorandum book with details of all the people he should meet with in Europe, as well as his own notes about how to approach them. He wrote these in a particular shorthand that only he could translate, in case it fell into the wrong hands. He also placed all the letters of introduction and credentials proving him an agent of the government into a small bag with a bit of lead to weight it down, and kept those things on him at all times.

These precautions proved prescient when, only thirty miles off the coast, an English corsair approached the *Johnston* and Royal officers claimed the right to board. Filippo immediately moved to the other side of the ship, slipped his memorandum book into the bag with the other illicit materials, and dropped them overboard. The incriminating papers sank out of sight. Filippo saw Captain Peyton shake hands with the English officer as he boarded, and when he heard the captain say, "I expected you yesterday morning," Filippo knew he had been right to mistrust Peyton.

The Mazzei party was removed to the corsair and taken to Sir George Collier, commander of the English fleet at New York. The women were sent to a local hotel while Collier grilled Filippo on the reasons for his visit to Europe, all the while hinting at it being a government mission that Collier himself might condone.

"Believe me," Collier kept repeating, "I've seen the resolve on the faces of the men in your military. They intend to win, and I intend to be on the right side when that happens."

"As do I," said Filippo, being just as vague about which side was the right side.

"My sources tell me you are a man of high respect in this colony," Collier said, taking a different tack. "A man entrusted with much."

Filippo played up his difficulty with the language, which enhanced his appearance of confusion over the whole affair, and kept to the story of needing to return to Italy for his own family and business needs. "I have done...how do you say...well?"

Collier nodded.

"Well, yes, well here in business. But," Filippo paused to play it up, "as you know, as you well know?"

Again, Collier instinctively nodded as one does to keep a conversation going.

"As you well know," Filippo continued, "now is it a difficult time for import and export concern such as mine, what with the waters so fraught with, well...things such as this as happened to me, a thing delaying my return to my homeland and to my business conducted there, yes?"

"But if you are headed to Tuscany, why did you take passage on a boat to France?"

"No boat was taking as timely a trip to Livorno—Leghorn, to you English."

"So you have no papers upon you for these...business dealings you are embarking upon on the continent, favors to do for Jefferson...or Washington?" Collier asked, convinced that Filippo had something that would allow the commander to show he had caught a spy.

"You do me too much honor, good sir, to think men of such station would ask me to assist in their...efforts." Filippo caught himself before defining the efforts as "noble" and giving Collier reason to further suspect him. He turned to the officer standing guard at the door. "I have a box of papers in my cabin, letters from my workers to their families back home. I will be pleased to open it in front of Sir Collier to clarify the reasons for my trip."

When his trunk arrived, Filippo opened it and displayed the letters and ledgers of work at Colle that proved him a normal planter concerned only with the planting and harvesting of his various products. Filippo noted that a letter from George Mason to his son in Europe was missing, but he thought better than to mention it and illustrate a loyalty to one of the known leaders of the Revolution. Luckily, the letter said nothing of their work together, merely being a missive of love from a father to a son.

Frustrated at finding no immediate evidence to hold Filippo, Collier released him to the officer of the corsair, only long enough for Filippo and his party to be taken to the prison warden in New York. There Filippo paid for his family's upkeep at an expensive rate, needing to solicit an advance from his relatives in Livorno to be paid back when he arrived on the continent—*if* he ever arrived on the continent.

The only light during their days was making the acquaintance of a young officer of Scottish descent whose parents had relocated to South Carolina. When war broke out, the gentleman had been torn. Having taken an oath to the king, he felt duty-bound to honor it, and he had, at the expense of losing connection to his parents. In their absence he had married a French widow with three children to create his own new instant family. Knowing Filippo had married a French widow with a child, he brought his family to visit Mrs. Martin and Maria, often providing that necessary hope for a better future when the war ended.

To cut back on expenses, and to be placed in a part of the city teeming with patriots to the United States without giving that as the reason, Filippo asked to meet with General Sir Henry Clinton, British commander in chief in North America, stationed at New York. Filippo had heard through his contacts that Clinton complained of the expenses of living in the city and Filippo planned to play on their mutual complaint.

Though Clinton's schedule did not allow a face-to-face meeting, his aide-de-camp arrived to meet with Filippo and providence seemingly took over the situation. The aide was none other than Lord Cathcart, whose father had been a good friend to Filippo in his time in London. His mere title of "Lord" carried with it the news that his father had died. He informed Filippo that his mother was gone as well.

"I want you to know I am more deeply moved by the loss of your parents than I have been since the death of my own father," Filippo said as they embraced in greeting.

Cathcart arranged for Filippo, Mrs. Martin, Maria, and Francesco to move to Long Island, New York, where the fees for their detention would be less and, as Filippo had been told, the population veered more toward Patriots than Tories. His new temporary neighbors had read Furioso's essays and knew of Filippo's deep connection to the Continental Congress—and to Jefferson—from conversations at inns across the colonies. While they spoke of the business that called him home, several did so with a wink in their eye toward his other mission, but Filippo never made any move to credit their suspicions in order to keep his cover solid and his family safe. He had quickly learned that one spy never quite recognized the other spies around them.

The locals honored Filippo for being a prisoner in the war for their own independence by charging him minimal fees for a maximum of comfort in his lodgings. To prove their loyalty to their fledgling country, they took Filippo to the secret location where, every Saturday evening, the local farmers and fishermen buried the money they made that week to avoid it being pillaged if the English won the war.

Filippo passed the time reading, writing, and taking long walks, looking only as irritated as a man being detained from his business should look, hoping to curb the concept of him as a spy. All the while, he received information on the side from other known Patriots about the meetings taking place regarding his case and if there was enough proof to court-martial him for treason to the king. Here having served on the Committee of Safety and not in the House of Burgesses did him well, though being such a known friend to Jefferson and Franklin did not.

One clandestine report claimed that a young Scottish officer stationed in New York had spoken favorably toward Filippo in his testimony, quite sure he could not be a spy. Yet another story from the court said that officers who had been stationed in Virginia felt Jefferson and Mazzei were the biggest rebels in the colonies.

"Yes, he did say that," said Filippo's informant. "In fact, he went so far as to say you and Jefferson deserved to be thrown into the sea, tied hands and feet to the same anchor."

"How did the court take that testimony?" Filippo asked.

"Well, sir," said his informant, a sailor who stood guard at a meeting or two. "Well, sir, that self-same young Scotsman demanded satisfaction."

"A duel? Over my honor?" asked Filippo incredulously.

"Yes, sir," said the informant. "And that Scotsman turned out to be quite a crack shot. He's fine, but that other officer'll be laid up in bed for a month."

"Will he live?" asked Filippo, sad that anyone would die over his name.

"Yes, sir, he will," said the informant. "That's what the doctors say. Your friend bein' such a good shot, he made sure it was a woundin' and not a killin'."

Apparently news of the duel traveled among the ladies' sewing circles as well as in the local pubs, as Mrs. Martin questioned Filippo about the incident over dinner that night, giving voice to concerns he had been trying to keep to himself so as not to worry Maria.

"What will become of us if you are jailed...or killed?" Mrs. Martin asked.

"Passage would be paid for you and Maria to reach France," Filippo said. "Your sister there can keep you until my estates would be settled and the funds transferred."

"Don't talk of estates," Maria said sincerely. "I can't bear the thought of losing you."

"Would we never return to Colle?" asked Mrs. Martin. Clearly she preferred being the mistress of her own estate to being the guest of her sister.

"At this moment, it is unclear if any of us will ever return to Colle," Filippo said tersely.

His obvious sadness at the thought of losing all he had built in Virginia quieted all conversation for the duration of dinner. Maria excused herself early and Filippo and Mrs. Martin finished their meal in silence.

The testimony of the Scotsman and others who had met and befriended Filippo along the way prevailed, and after three months the case was closed. General Clinton gave the

Mazzei party permission to leave for Europe, and they did so immediately in order to avoid any other entanglements. Filippo arranged passage on the first boat leaving for Europe, even though its destination, Cork, Ireland, had not been on his agenda. Leaving suspicions behind in New York and being in a place where he could begin making the connections needed to fund the Continental Army made heading for Cork the best course of action.

Sadly, as with all ocean voyages Filippo endured over his lifetime, this one, too, made him nauseous to the point of constant vomiting. As always, he managed to feel fine for the first few days, dining with the others and walking the decks for air during the day, but within a week he was bedridden by both seasickness and a bout of fever that held on for more than ten days. During that time, Maria administered to him as a daughter should a father, while Mrs. Martin spent the bulk of her time on deck reading, resenting all the while that she'd had to leave her little fiefdom. Sometimes Filippo had the feeling she was sorry he hadn't been executed so she could live the life of an independent widow.

The voyage turned slightly better only when a young, educated French officer came on board and spent afternoons telling Filippo all the news of Europe, which was quite useful to his mission. War had been declared between England and the House of Bourbon, so the king's men were now fighting on two fronts, which would weaken their power in America. It was handy news for Filippo to send back to Washington at the first opportunity.

After forty days, their ship arrived at Cork, and the representative of the line, Mr. Cotter, greeted Filippo and his party enthusiastically. The Irish, being second-class citizens to the English and having sent many of their young people to the New

World as indentured servants, felt a deep fondness for America and its people. Cotter arranged for comfortable lodgings for Filippo's group, which came in most handy when Filippo discovered the bill of exchange he had brought from America was no longer valid. After being forced to pay so much for the berths on the *Johnston* and then for lodgings in New York while a prisoner, Filippo had only the gold watch he had given Mrs. Martin and Maria when they first left England for America, and the one matching one he held. He offered those to their landlord to sell, but Cotter intervened.

"You must tell me when you need assistance," Cotter pleaded. "I am not a rich man, but sharing with you now will not ruin me, and you will cause me real displeasure if you do not accept my contribution to the cause of American independence."

Filippo knew Cotter had no knowledge of Filippo's actual assignment, but merely wanted to be a part of a greater victory. Filippo understood that desire and graciously accepted, making a note for repayment at a later date.

Cotter handed Filippo some letters that had arrived on other boats, with the happy news that Jefferson had been elected governor of Virginia and moved the capital city from Williamsburg, then more vulnerable to British attack by sea, to Richmond, which also happened to be half the distance from Monticello as Williamsburg was.

Likewise, Maria received a letter from the new First Lady of the state, Martha Jefferson, inquiring into her health and happiness on the trip, and detailing a drive among the women of Virginia to raise funds and supplies for her state's militia in response to a request from Martha Washington.

"I wish I was there to help her," Maria said out loud.

"I wish we were all there," Mrs. Martin snapped back.

Then Maria realized such a remark might sound like a complaint and quickly rescinded it. "I only meant that Mrs. Jefferson's health permits her very little exertion and I hope this war work will not take too heavy a toll on her."

"I am sure if you were there, you would be a great help to Mrs. Jefferson," Filippo said pointedly to Maria, but not to Mrs. Martin. While he managed to maintain a civil relationship with his wife in public, in private things had become much tenser since his talk with Jefferson and Bellini. His peace would come when they reached France and she could be left behind at the home of her sister in Calais, an event not far away, as that day he had procured passage on a Portuguese ship headed for Nantes. They boarded the next night in a hurry so that no one would recognize Filippo and question his interest in France.

"You might end up in the Tower of London, never to descend," said Cotter, who came to see them off and keep an eye out for spies. He was referencing another American, Henry Laurens, former president of the Continental Congress, who had negotiated Dutch support for the war. On his way back home with the paperwork, the British intercepted his ship. Like Filippo, Laurens tossed his papers overboard, but unlike Filippo, he hadn't had the forethought to weight them down—so the British retrieved the papers, used them to charge Laurens with treason, and imprisoned him in the Tower of London. Laurens only earned release as an exchange for General Lord Cornwallis.

"I'll take my chances," Filippo said. "With men like you on our side, we can't help but win."

"And if not?" asked Cotter.

"If not, we go down trying," said Filippo.

The men embraced and Filippo ascended the ladder after Mrs. Martin and Maria were safely aboard. Francesco followed him and the boat set sail.

Several times a day Filippo heard his own words "we go down trying" echo in his brain as the ship and its crew turned out to be disturbingly dilapidated. Among the other passengers were three young priests bound for Rome and a Catholic mother and daughter, all of whom spent days saying rosaries to survive the wind and squall. Filippo found himself bedridden yet again. Still, these other passengers came to him daily for his opinion on the success of their voyage as he was the most educated man on board—so educated that he soon realized the captain had overshot their landing and was losing control of the ship in the high winds. The only crewmen Filippo found to be at all useful were two young men from Calais. That night he gathered the others together for what essentially became a passenger mutiny.

"Without the hard work all night of these two intelligent seamen, we would all be food for the fishes today," he began. "It is clear to me that the captain and pilot believe this tacking about will finally reach land, but they have brought us no closer to land, only closer to crashing into the rocks. If we have to spend another night on the sea, we will be lost."

"What can we do besides pray?" asked one of the priests.

"I propose we pray," said Filippo, "but I also propose we act. We call the captain and insist instead of his intended landing, he take us to the island of Rhé, which can be seen with the naked eye and for which route we would have the wind at our back."

Using Filippo's plan, the passengers made it to Rhé, off the coast of France. They spent one night in a local lodge and dispersed the following day—some to Rome, some to nearby La

Rochelle, and Filippo and his party to Nantes, arriving at the end of November, 1779. By now the war for American independence had been raging for three years and Filippo was anxious to get to work.

Chapter Fourteen

REPRESENTING HIS NEW COUNTRY IN FRANCE

Nantes proved disappointing. Filippo found himself still short on operating cash and none of the papers confirming his commission or further detailing his instructions had yet arrived, such that his ability to meet with leaders was severely infringed. The best course of action was to move on to Paris, where he could encounter a delegation of Americans with knowledge of his mission, and so his now very tired party traveled onward. Mrs. Martin had descended into an impossible companion. It was from Paris that Filippo had promised to send her and Maria on to her sister in Calais, but Mrs. Martin kept finding reasons not to leave quite yet. Filippo had to maneuver around town doing clandestine business and return to the hotel at night to hear how she had voiced her disapproval of him as a husband to all who would listen. He feared it might hinder his ability to meet with some important men in Europe, but was heartened by what Benjamin Franklin had to say in their first meeting since their days in London.

They met at Franklin's residence in Auteuil, on the west side of Paris, but could not speak frankly about Filippo's commission until the previously invited dinner guest, Dr.

Ingenhousz, had finished dinner and departed. Until then, they discussed Ingenhousz's recent encounters with the grand duke at Tuscany and the emperor with whom he crossed paths in Milan. Ingenhousz wanted to focus on gossip concerning the grand duke, but Franklin and Filippo were far more interested in the science of inoculation, as inoculating the duke's children had been the doctor's business in Tuscany. Since 1774, when Franklin founded the Society for Inoculating the Poor Gratis, he had been an eloquent advocate for the practice, and for making it affordable to the poor, as the high expense of inoculations kept most of the public from having them.

"A ridiculous mistake for those in the upper incomes, as once infections and epidemics take hold of a town, they do not skip houses merely because one family has more money in the bank than the other," Franklin ranted. It was his table and his right to rant if he so chose, Filippo felt. Normally, Franklin held such vehement talk for his editorials, but Filippo knew inoculation was a personal issue for his friend. In 1736, the Franklins lost their youngest son to smallpox at the age of four. Franklin had foregone inoculation as his older brother, James Franklin, argued in the press that inoculation was a breach of the Sixth Commandment, "Thou shalt not kill." But when his own son was lost, Franklin forewent protecting his brother's stance and came out for the procedure.

"It has been proven to work in most studies on the subject," Filippo said. "We used it at Santa Nuova, and Franklin and I know John Adams inoculated his whole family against the Boston epidemic of '76."

"Hell," Franklin injected, "Washington ordered his soldiers to be inoculated last year because more men were falling to smallpox than to Redcoat muskets."

"Agreed," said Ingenhousz.

"Odd that Europe—and Asia—would be more comfortable with the practice than such a forward-thinking place as America," mused Filippo. "When I was in Smyrna, inoculation was common practice. "

"You know as well as I do…perhaps more so since you have chosen to live among our Southern brethren and that perfidious practice…you know that anything with a hint of proving the slaves they treat as property are actually human beings—human beings with histories and intellects—is anathema among your neighbors," Franklin said.

He didn't have to mention Jefferson by name. Filippo knew this question of slavery had been injecting itself into their friendship for years, each man having a different definition of what American independence might mean.

"But even they can't deny the truth," Filippo said. "Even the great Cotton Mather credited the slave who taught him inoculation when he began speaking about the need for expanding the practice. In my studies I often heard that together Onesimus and Mather saved many, many a Bostonian in that awful epidemic."

"They can deny whatever they care to deny, whatever stands in the way of their irrational belief in their own superiority. We aren't as forward thinking as you suppose," Franklin admitted. "But we're working on it. Once this war is over, imagine what we can do."

Once Ingenhousz bid them farewell after cigars, Franklin and Filippo could avidly begin the discussion of what each could do to help win this war. But Franklin was not as happy as expected about Filippo's commission.

"Foreign affairs ought to be left to the care of Congress," Franklin began. "Virginia must realize it is part of a larger collective now, not its own country, or what are we fighting for?"

"Virginia has provided us our commander in chief," Filippo said. "It is in Virginia's best interest to make sure the commander has all he needs to prosecute this war or the idea of a collective country is no more than a dream. Right now the highest funding comes from Virginia, Massachusetts—"

"And Pennsylvania. Don't forget Pennsylvania."

"How could I? It is at the heart of all that we are doing. But there are more loyalist lands to confiscate—and sell to fund the army—in Virginia than anywhere else right now, so we are raising more funds faster."

"Yes, but more war bonds are being sold in Pennsylvania, Massachusetts, and Connecticut than in Virginia," Franklin argued. Defending his home state had always been an admirable trait of his.

"Be that as it may," Filippo said, "aid of any kind is of the greatest need and value right now, so what does it hurt if there are several agents from several organizations out and about soliciting for the badly needed funds?"

"It's true. Each agent offers different contacts on this continent, and you offer, perhaps, the best."

"You flatter me, sir, unnecessarily. I have already committed to the task."

"Yes, I could have guessed you would do what you could for our country," Franklin said.

Filippo smiled inwardly at the idea of Franklin willing to share ownership in America.

Franklin continued, "And you move so well in the sorts of circles where the money and power we need connect lives. I welcome you to the task."

From that dinner onward Filippo spent his time meeting old friends and creating new ones for the colonies by writing articles such as "Why the American States Cannot Be Called Rebels," "The Importance of Commerce in Virginia," and "The Justice of the American Cause." Of particular interest were the letters he wrote both privately and publicly in the newspapers addressed to several leaders in France and Italy, explaining the benefits those countries would reap if they took advantage of the moment and supported the fledgling country. Difficulties arose from the fact that his commission papers were held up on the other side of the ocean, so he had no formal proof he could offer such benefits or foster the proper diplomatic relationships.

The Marquis Domenico Caracciolo, an old friend who served as the diplomatic representative for the Kingdom of Naples in Paris, believed Filippo without written proof. Caracciolo threw the kinds of parties that attracted many important diplomats and politicians for the fine wine and food, and for Caracciolo himself, who was known as a delightful conversationalist. Caracciolo saw the benefits for Italy of supporting the Americans against the English and spread that message at all his events.

Soon Caracciolo was in an even better position to help Filippo, though it felt like it would hurt Caracciolo. While dining with Filippo one night and planning yet another party, Caracciolo received word that he had been promoted to viceroy to the Kingdom of Sicily.

"Congratulations, my friend!" said Filippo heartily when Caracciolo opened the letter.

"*Si*, it is a compliment," Caracciolo said with a tinge of sadness. "But it means I must remove myself to Sicily when I enjoy the life here in Paris most especially."

To assuage his friend's feelings, Filippo reminded him, "Ah, yes, but I can see that your overindulgence of that enjoyment has caused your legs to swell, and as a former doctor I can tell you that the climate in Palermo will be much more suited to your health. The richness of the food here has done you harm. You need less cream and more vegetables in your diet."

"You are right about the legs, but the head counts for something, too," Caracciolo said. "If I could take with me a half a dozen people of my own choosing, I should be very happy, but that is out of the question."

Before Caracciolo left Paris, Filippo negotiated a business deal between America and Sicily to increase the amount of sulfur sent from the vast sulfur deposits in Sicily to the New World to help them manufacture gunpowder for the Continental Army. Caracciolo took Filippo at his word about his commission with no paper proof required and it helped other diplomats in Italy and France begin to do so as well.

Though Filippo was on business for the colonies, his natural curiosity and kindness prevailed when he met Valentin Haüy, a teacher who had created a system for teaching the blind to read and write. Among the many interesting people Filippo had come across in Paris that year, Haüy stood out immediately. Filippo first encountered the young man soliciting funds at a pub for the support of a school he was running, where he taught blind children to read by using wooden blocks with letters and numbers carved on them. The idea had come to him when he gave coins to a blind boy begging outside his local parish.

"The child felt the raised markings on the coin and knew it to be true currency," Haüy said to Filippo as he made his pitch for funding.

"And you thought that books could be made with raised letters," Filippo realized excitedly as they talked.

"That is exactly what I thought," said Haüy. "See? You feel the same sense of excitement at the possibility that I felt that day. And now, through my small school, I am teaching those who cannot see with their eyes to read…"

"With their fingers," Filippo finished the thought.

"From that time I have dedicated my life to the education of the blind. The children live together with me, study together with me, and work to keep the school neat and clean. Can you help us?"

Filippo felt awful at the fact that, due to all the confusion about his commission and his own funding, he had no spare funds to contribute. Instead, he offered Haüy his connections with dukes and various other nobles, many of whom found the idea of making men who were thought to be useless to society productive an enticing one. They gave generously and spread the word of Haüy's successes across Europe.

Filippo happily corresponded with Carlo Bellini, who through Jefferson's intercession as governor of Virginia and member of the Board of Visitors, had been granted the first-ever appointment as a professor of modern languages at the College of William and Mary. Then, just a year later, he became the college librarian. To increase the size of the library's collection, he wrote asking Filippo to send him as many books by ancient authors as he could lay hands on, as well as a few by modern European authors. Filippo did as requested and also informed Bellini of which American authors were being read in the various countries he visited.

In Filippo's correspondence with Jefferson, the men could not discuss business or politics at all on the event that the letters were opened by the English, so they discussed their first love, agriculture. There the good news involved Filippo sending Jefferson a shipment of choice Italian varieties of peaches and giving him permission to take cuttings of other exotic fruits he had sent back to Colle. Filippo learned that two of the peasants who came with him to Virginia had become deeply helpful to Jefferson, and to the new nation. Giovannini da Prato worked for Jefferson while he was serving as governor of Williamsburg and Richmond, and Antonio Giannini was with the Virginia militia in September and October of 1781, but called home to manage the gardens as they produced foodstuffs for the soldiers. Jefferson wrote that having Giannini take over the care of the Monticello orchard, performing the annual grafting and budding operations, reminded him of a passage Filippo had shared with him in Book Two of *The Georgics*, where Virgil celebrated the art of grafting by writing of the importance of taking the time to "soften the wild fruits by cultivating them."

Happily, when Antonio and Maria Giannini's second son, Francesco, was born, they gave him the middle name of Tomei—Italian for "Thomas"—in honor of an overjoyed Jefferson, who gifted the couple with forty-five gallons of whiskey in celebration of the birth. This news made Filippo proud of his friends, his home country, and his new country.

Sadly, bad news followed the good. Jefferson wrote that Riedesel, Filippo's renter, paid no mind to the grapevines at Colle and consequently his horses trampled them all. In Jefferson's words, "They destroyed the whole labor of three or four years, and thus ended an experiment, which, from every appearance, would in a year or two more have established the practicability of that branch of culture in America." Filippo barely had the chance to mourn the loss of so much time and work, so many shared hopes between himself and Jefferson, when worse news came—first in the war news in the local newspapers and then corroborated by Jefferson in a hastily scribbled letter, not his normal style at all.

General Benedict Arnold, once a hero to the Americans but now known to have defected to the English in a huff over not being granted a higher commission, had recently attacked Virginia. Washington warned Jefferson, in his position as governor of the state, to prepare. Jefferson rode for days around Richmond trying to organize resistance, but could not muster enough extra men into the militia. Some did not believe an attacking force could make it that far, others had already served, and still others felt the end of the war was just around the corner. Without enough troops, Virginia did not have a fighting chance when Arnold's ships approached Richmond via the James River. Arnold demanded the surrender of the one-year-old capital or he would torch the town.

"Naturally, Jefferson did not surrender," Filippo told Maria over breakfast one day when Mrs. Martin had remained in her bed with a headache. "A governor does not negotiate with turncoats."

"What of Mrs. Jefferson and the girls?" Maria asked.

"He escorted them to safety," Filippo assured her as he scanned the later paragraphs of the letter. "Though in their rush, he fell and broke his arm." Off Maria's worried face, he added,

"But it is mending. And as governor he sent fifteen tons of gunpowder out of the city, then he, too, fled to Monticello."

"Thank goodness," sighed Maria.

Filippo could not read her the rest of the letter at that time. It would wound her too much to learn that after Arnold's troops finished confiscating the tobacco stored in local warehouses, meant to be sold to fund the Virginia militia, the general let his troops ransack Richmond. He then sent a detachment led by British officer Banastre Tarleton, which arrived at Monticello and then Colle. There Arnold's men plundered both homes, cracked open many casks of wine, and burned the numerous wartime letters and documents they did not steal.

Maria saw the look on his face as he read silently. "What is it? They are all fine, yes?" she begged him to tell her.

"Yes, our friends are fine. Our homes have withstood some damage, but our people are fine. In fact, more than fine. The last person standing with Jefferson at Monticello was Antonio."

"*Madre mio.* Bless him," said Maria, crossing herself.

"And Caterina carried meals to the Jeffersons while they were in hiding from the troops," Filippo said with a smile as he remembered the two-year-old who had traveled across the ocean with her parents what seemed such a long time ago.

"And she's but eight by now."

"Yes, I imagine her parents knew the troops wouldn't bother with the daytime antics of a child, so she could easily have carried small baskets of food to them."

"Where did they hide?"

"He does not say."

"Perhaps because he fears the need to flee again?"

"Oh no," Filippo countered quickly to assuage her. "I believe he does not wish to cause any trouble to whoever helped him should this letter have been intercepted en route to us."

"Why did such a letter pass through?"

"I imagine it is to make sure we hear that the troops are wreaking havoc. To ruin our morale."

"Then I won't let it do so," promised Maria.

The only smile this event brought to their faces came from reading Bellini's reporting.

During the British occupation of Williamsburg, Bellini remained alone on the campus of William and Mary. When the French army finally arrived to push out the English and use the area to prepare for the battle of Yorktown in the fall of 1781, Bellini wined and dined the Frenchmen, who appreciated his ability to both speak French and to understand their customs. Bellini wrote that while he had been badly treated by the British, Arnold's troops did not ransack the college library, since it was named for British royalty.

Filippo did not share with Maria two other developments from these near-tragic events—news that came in other correspondence about the invasion, events he felt would have far-reaching effects. First, the Italian peasants stayed true to their employers while many enslaved people took the opportunity to escape, with some joining the British troops to work as cooks or valets. This proved Filippo's oft-repeated stance that the system of slave labor on which Virginia thrived could not survive. Second, Jefferson wrote that he intended to step down as governor that summer. Filippo's friends reported that Jefferson had fallen into a deep depression. The stress of hiding and the fear of what might happen to them had weakened their sixteen-month-old daughter, Lucy, and she died just two weeks later. Maria had exchanged letters with Mrs. Jefferson during the pregnancy and had embroidered a layette for the child that had yet to be posted. He had no idea how he was going to tell her this news.

All these other issues did not detract Filippo from his original mission; in fact, the news of Arnold's attack made him even more motivated to succeed. Since that mission required moving throughout the countries of Europe to secure as much support as possible, Filippo quickly made plans to depart for Florence by way of Lyons and Genoa. First, he arranged for any of his future mail to be delivered to Franklin, so that the commission papers would not fall into the wrong hands. Next, he sent some letters directly to the address he expected to occupy in Florence, letters with false information about how the war was going and what Filippo was doing in Europe, hoping that if the letters were intercepted, they would further confuse the English.

Last, Filippo had to finally deal with Mrs. Martin, who had managed to lengthen her stay in Paris this long. When she refused to go to her sister's home yet again, Filippo left enough funds for lodging and food for one more month, plus enough to pay for the trip to Calais. He had no emotion except relief at their parting.

With Maria, by contrast, he had a tearful goodbye. For all intents and purposes, she was the only child he had ever had.

Chapter Fifteen

FINDING FRIENDS AND FAMILY IN ITALY

Filippo's frustration deepened as he traveled through Lyons and Genoa in 1782, staying for only short periods as his formal papers still did not arrive. He could only present himself and his mission to previous friends, as he had with Caracciolo, who would trust him at his word. That happened in Florence, where he requested and received a private audience with the grand duke from his advisor Angiolo Tavanti, himself one of Fillipo's old friends.

"I can only divulge the purpose of my visit to the two of you alone," Filippo told Tavanti.

"Only to the grand duke," said Tavanti. "He prefers to have sole knowledge of your reasons for this visit, suspecting, as I do, that politics is at the heart of it."

"How so?"

"We have been privy to information from the post office that the British confiscated several letters sent to you in our city."

Filippo thanked Tavanti for that information, but in deference to the duke's request, did not let Tavanti know those were the letters he had written with false information, intending to fool the king. He smiled to himself that his plan had worked.

Tavanti then leaned in to whisper his own confidence before the duke entered the chamber. "You should know that the duke often boasts of being more informed on the American situation than anyone else in Europe, and he never reveals the source of that information."

The grand duke entered the room with words of praise for Filippo's foresight on his lips. "There is no doubt that you predicted everything that has come to pass." He and Filippo embraced.

"Then you must believe me when I tell you that my mail has been seized, and I know who decreed it," Filippo said, and the duke nodded for him to continue. "I suspect Sir Horace Mann."

Filippo knew Mann was most beloved by the locals as he had been an English diplomat in Tuscany since 1737. Great Britain had no diplomatic representation at Rome, so Mann's duties included reporting on the activities of the British royal exiles of the Stuart dynasty, making him yet closer to the royal family. So Filippo treaded lightly in his accusation, but made it just the same.

"I have heard the things he says about the English victories in America, and though he is incapable of lying voluntarily, his blind faith in the English government does not serve him well in this instance," Filippo said.

Off the duke's look of incredulity, Filippo continued. "I intend to prove it on this trip so that his influence will fade and support for the Americans will rise, at least here in Tuscany. Will you allow me that chance?"

Always a smart man, the duke agreed to let Filippo see if he could prove Mann's part in seizing his letters, but he also instructed that from that point on, all mail intended for Filippo was to be delivered immediately to the palace, into his hands.

Meanwhile, they arranged that Filippo would meet with Mann at breakfast in his gardens at the Palazzo Manetti the next morning.

Filippo and Mann shared a friendship from Filippo's first time in Florence, when Mann was being ostracized for his close friendship to Thomas Patch, a painter expelled from Rome after a report of his involvement in homosexual activities. Filippo had stood by Mann then, when few other Catholics had. Now they were on separate sides of a conflict that Filippo's presence here was trying to turn global. How would he be received? Did Mann already suspect the secret commission? Did he intercept the papers that described Filippo's commission? All these questions flooded Filippo's thoughts as he entered the grounds of the palazzo.

Mann met him alone at the door and took his hand, clearly unsure of where Filippo stood and what exactly to say.

Filippo filled the silence. "Sir, I know there is much in your heart which you cannot put into words. After such a long absence, to see a dear friend again…"

"At this time I am not my own master," Mann finally said.

He kissed Filippo's hand and Filippo tactfully took his leave. There was nothing either could safely say and, sadly, they never saw each other again.

Filippo dedicated his time to writing more essays for the foreign press and traveled to Livorno to visit his cousins Domenico and Vincenzo. Filippo proudly observed how their store thrived due to the exchange of goods entered into during his time in England and then America.

"This is a miniature of how Italy herself will thrive if she supports the Americans in this war," Vincenzo said one day at dinner.

He looked at Filippo, expecting his cousin to admit his true reason for returning to Europe, but Filippo's theory was the fewer who knew for sure, the fewer who would be made to pay the price if the colonies did not win the war. While Filippo could not make formal deals with government officials without the required paperwork, he could and did write articles for *Notizie del Mundo,* an opposition paper against the *Gazzeta,* which only published official English news. Filippo's essays provided another perspective on the conflict and helped change attitudes toward the Continental Congress and its goals.

On the second day of Filippo's visit, Domenico told him that a mysterious foreign woman required an audience and asked him to grant the request. When they arrived together at the local Malta Inn, Filippo discovered the mystery woman's identity: Mrs. Martin. She threw her arms around the naive Domenico and exclaimed, "My dear cousin!" in thanks until Filippo pulled them apart gently.

"If you are here, where is Maria?" Filippo asked brusquely.

"I could not leave Paris until she had made a suitable match—"

"You married her off without telling me?" Filippo interrupted. He was not annoyed at the fact that she hadn't consulted him. He understood he was not her biological father, but Filippo had always felt such warmth toward her, he had imagined attending her wedding himself someday. Mrs. Martin's actions denied him that honored privilege.

As they held their tense conversation, Filippo learned that Mrs. Martin had used the money meant for Calais to stay on in

Paris until the courtship was completed. Maria married Mr. de Rieux, oldest son of the Countess de Jaucourt, despite a lack of papers from Virginia attesting to her unmarried status, so the Marquis Caracciolo had agreed to stand as a guarantor. Mrs. Martin claimed the French king approved the match, and further, had created a noble title for Filippo in its honor.

Filippo could see that Domenico, being less traveled and therefore less sophisticated than Filippo, believed every word. His cousin was therefore shocked when Filippo dismissed Mrs. Martin with an introduction to a boarding house in Pisa and a letter of credit to cover expenses, and bid her as polite a goodbye as he could manage.

For a second time Mrs. Martin went on to break their verbal contract. As Filippo prepared to move on to Holland to make more connections, she returned to Florence, claiming Pisa bored her. Filippo had done his homework now via a series of letters to her sister, and understood why Mrs. Martin kept avoiding Calais. Her sister had married into one of the best families in the city and raised Mrs. Martin when their own mother died young. However, that arrogant, affected, and overall prickly personality that Filippo's Virginia friends deplored so had served her no better in Calais. A need to escape a lack of suitors caused her rash early marriage to the lesser-respected Martin family. So returning to the control of that older sister, and the long simmering dislike that still existed in Calais, kept her away from the city. To counter that, this time Filippo left the money for her move to Calais with his old friend Raimondo Cocchi, with instructions not to give it to Mrs. Martin for any other expenses except travel to Calais.

Filippo tried to explain to Domenico why Mrs. Martin deserved only a terse recognition of her station as his wife, since they had never lived completely as man and wife. The conversation came on the heels of a letter to Filippo announcing the sad news of the death of Rami Kadın, his old friend from the court of Mahmud I, and her royal burial in Mahmudpaşa Mosque, Istanbul.

"*This* was a woman," Filippo explained to Domenico. "A woman who lived in a situation not of her choosing, but who found a way to make life better for all around her. On a daily basis. Would that my legal wife would have looked upon her situation with as much magnitude, for her situation was far superior to being a concubine among many."

He was surprised to learn that Domenico's naive nature ran to the point where Filippo had to explain the duties of a concubine.

"Naturally, I have heard such stories," Domenico said, "but thought them stories, such as the ones told by Carlo Collodi or…or Dante."

Filippo assured Domenico that real life inspired many stories, including those of Ali Baba and the Forty Thieves. Then he sat down to write a letter of condolence to Mahmud I, who in Filippo's mind had lost a great companion in life. After losing his beloved grandfather and knowing his mother preferred his unkind brother over him, few things made Filippo more sad than knowing he would likely never share such a match in his life as Mahmud had with Rami.

In that mood, Filippo then traveled to Amsterdam via Tyrol, Trent, and Frankfort, taking time to enjoy cultural events at each stop, including choirs who performed in churches across his trip. They lifted his spirits and reenergized him in his efforts for the new government he had helped to usher into America. Several of the most successful merchants in the city came to meet Filippo on the word of John Adams, who was then at The Hague on his own first trip to Europe as a representative of the United States. Though they had not yet met in person, Adams had read Filippo's essays and trusted the words of Jefferson and Franklin. Adams spread the word about Filippo's mission and his good character, thus opening doors for Filippo's work. Two important brothers in Amsterdam, Nicholas and Jacob van Staphorst, wrote letters of introduction for Filippo into the finest circles, and even letters back to banks in Paris guaranteeing any monies he would need to continue his work. As with most of his new acquaintances, the brothers became his friends for life.

Filippo returned to Paris a few days after the peace delegation from the United States, which included John Adams, Benjamin Franklin, and Henry Laurens. They had succeeded in having King George's advisors sign the preliminaries of peace, an amazing outcome as no colony had ever broken from its mother country in the past.

In Paris, Filippo often took long walks with Adams. Among the shops and along the Champs-Élysées they walked, arguing politely over what Filippo thought were Adams's mistaken principles. On their last day together, Filippo summed it up by saying, "I hope we shall see each other again in America, perhaps in Boston. Above all, I should consider it a duty to seek you out in order to combat your views because they produce effects as injurious as your merits are praiseworthy. You have the advantage of eloquence in a language of which you have so much better command than I, but I have the advantage of being in the right."

Filippo met with all the other delegates from the States as well, including John Jay of New York. While they all had various complaints against Adams, they all had the same complaint against Franklin.

"He basks in the celebrity of being the one true American," Jay said. "Wearing that damnable fur cap and jutting about town as though he is the only American on the continent."

"Well, our friend has always been fond of the attention of the ladies," Filippo said in slight defense of Franklin.

"The ladies, yes," said Jay. "But now he wants everyone to notice him and only him. It's unbecoming to a man of his age. What is he making them all think about us as Americans?"

"He's making them think about us," Filippo said. "And right now that is quite an important goal, for we will need friends, loans, and other assistance to find our footing in the world."

"Well," conceded Jay, "the least he could do was present the rest of us to court. He holds that privilege but refuses to wield it, preferring to keep the limelight to himself."

On behalf of Jay and the other visiting diplomats, Filippo spoke discreetly to Franklin about arranging court appearances for all of them, but Franklin had a pat answer ready.

"I have only so much clout to spread around in the name of our new country," he said. "I shall not waste it inviting every man who wants to shake the hand of a royal in for the privilege. We are supposed to be proving monarchy is not the way to govern."

"I agree on that count," Filippo said. "But even without our own monarchy, we will have to deal with the monarchies around us in as delicate a way as possible, proving our leadership is on equal footing with theirs. How else can you do that without introducing the two?"

Franklin took Filippo's idea and molded it to his own philosophy. "I shall introduce some men into court, but to prove the power of the vote, they shall be men elected into their positions, not merely those appointed. That will demonstrate the differences in our governing systems."

While this conversation did nothing to help Jay gain presentation in court since his was an appointed commission, it accidentally helped Filippo, who had been elected to the Committee of Safety and therefore fulfilled Franklin's requirements. In truth, Filippo also knew that Franklin hoped to build a network of supporters for America—and for himself—out of the friends Filippo had already engaged. Among the guests at Filippo's presentation dinner, Franklin particularly enjoyed meeting the Marquis Caracciolo and learning of his earlier exploits with Filippo.

Filippo would have stayed longer in Paris to join in the festivities surrounding the signing of the peace treaty, truly a once-in-a-lifetime experience, but word came that once again Mrs. Martin had not gone to Calais, but instead to the home of the Count de Jaucourt, where Maria shared rooms with her new husband, his stepson. So Filippo set off for Toulouse by the roundabout route that took him first to the Canal of Languedoc, about a hundred kilometers to the east of Toulouse. Should anyone in America plan to build canals to facilitate trade and commerce, Filippo wanted a firsthand study of how they worked.

The detour also gave him the chance to learn as much as he could about the family of his stepdaughter. Sadly, this news disturbed him greatly. While word among the gentry spoke well of the conduct of Maria's husband, it turned out her mother-in-law had squandered her first husband's ancient fortune and had a head start on wasting away what belonged to the count. Apparently, Mrs. Martin had assured this lady that Filippo had inherited a fortune and already willed it all to Maria. He smiled slightly at the thought that both these mothers-in-law had believed the other's lies, but felt deeply wounded that such a lie had been perpetrated in his name and that it had put Maria and her husband in a tenuous financial position.

After collecting all this information, his only course of action was to write to the count to say he would come to his home—on the condition that Filippo's wife be sent on to Calais so that they would not need to cross paths. He explained their standing agreement, which she had continued to break, and declared he wanted nothing further to do with her. While he was still observing the canal, Filippo received the count's response, which promised Mrs. Martin had been sent on her way, so Filippo went to visit Maria.

There he learned that, while the mothers had been trading lies, the couple had told each other the truth of their finances and were happy with each other as mates. Neither Filippo nor the count, whom he came to enjoy as a dear friend, was in a position to assist them presently.

"But when I return to Virginia, I shall find some employ-ment for Mr. de Rieux and send you both home on my expense," Filippo promised. He felt a warmth come over him when he saw the smile come to Maria's face at the mention of "home" and he, too, realized how much he missed Colle—and Monticello, and all of Virginia. He had not realized when he undertook this commission that it would require distancing himself from the land he loved for such a long time. He immediately began to make plans to return.

Before those plans were carried out, Filippo decided it would be useful to visit with merchants in Bordeaux, France, as becom-ing acquainted with them would help facilitate trading with the merchants back in Virginia. After the war, the most important way to stabilize the new country would be through commerce with other friendly countries and the collection of taxes to support the new government.

Unhappily, but not surprisingly, Mrs. Martin appeared in Bordeaux, having not yet traveled to Calais, but by now enough of Filippo's associates knew the true story of their arrangement. When he refused to receive her, no one was surprised. It continued to be a sad spot in Filippo's otherwise successful travels in the name of his adopted country, and it haunted him as he headed back home.

Chapter Sixteen

RETURNING TO HIS ADOPTED COUNTRY

Filippo arrived back in his beloved Virginia in November 1783, happy to have been recalled by the new governor, Benjamin Harrison, but troubled by several immediate events. First, as his ship landed at the Hampton dock, he learned Jefferson had just left for Boston en route to France to serve as Franklin's replacement as America's representative in that country. Franklin's resignation came from his desire to, as he wrote Filippo, "end my days in my own country." Filippo immediately wrote a phalanx of letters to his various contacts in France, avowing that, while they all felt Franklin would be a great loss to their circle, Jefferson would make a worthy replacement.

The next day Filippo went to the new governor to make a complete account of his mission, delivering all contacts, business agreements, and notes of all his meetings, only to find that no record of his commission—or the honorarium due him for his work—existed. Since the mission had been devised as a secret one, few men knew about it at all. The English had burned many buildings along the way and most men who had served the state government in its genesis had retired to estates elsewhere. At the council meeting that the governor called to decide what to do, the men requested that Filippo procure letters from those earlier officials detailing how much he was allowed to promise and how much he should be paid.

Luckily, a letter from Jefferson in Boston came quickly and told Filippo where in Monticello hidden letters to that effect could be found. He also wrote Filippo of the true reason he was willing to take on Franklin's post and leave the country quickly, which meant leaving behind his beloved Monticello for several years: Martha Jefferson had died a few months after a difficult childbirth. Jefferson's letter to Filippo described how "a single event wiped away all my plans and left me a blank which I had not the spirits to fill up," and articulated his need to get away from "the state of dreadful suspense in which I had been kept all the summer and the catastrophe which closed it." He could not bear to be surrounded by all those things that reminded him of her and all the time he had been away from her on government business, never knowing their time together would be so short. Filippo had no idea how he would write this tragic news to Maria.

To prove his position and secure his salary—badly needed now that Colle was producing so much less thanks to Riedesel and his damnable vine-crushing horses—Filippo embarked on a series of visits with the men who had designed his commission. Many were now scattered across the state, living on land granted them by the new government in exchange for their service during the war, since the government didn't have enough money to make proper recompense.

Madison, the youngest of the state councilors who had been in meetings arranging Filippo's assignment, now resided nearest, in his father's home at Montpelier. As the plantation was next door to Monticello, about a day's ride from Colle, Filippo rode through the old vineyards on his way to Monticello. There he took time to confer with Giannini and da Prato, who were still living in Mulberry Row. Together the three men shared a bottle of wine hidden from the ransackers and Filippo thanked them profusely for their loyalty to his endeavor. Though they had more time in the contracts of their indentures, Filippo thought it proper to reward that loyalty by registering them as completed, and paying the men with the land promised them in their contracts.

"I am only sorry that thanks to Riedesel's idiocy, the land is not in the condition I hoped to have before granting you both your lots," Filippo said.

"No reason to apologize," Giannini said immediately. "You are a man of your word and we thank you for that."

"Besides," added da Prato, "as you always say, men work harder on their own land. I think there might be a bit still salvaged from that man's occupancy."

"I'm happy to hear it," Filippo said. "You can pick your lots based on what you'd most like to cultivate, be you wheat men or tobacco men or vintners."

"Would that you could make this offer to some of the others here on Mulberry Row," Giannini said.

"Like you predicted," said da Prato, "several of them ran to the English when they could, but that lot gave them nothing much, so they came back."

"But others, like that James Hemings—he stayed and protected the stores in the kitchen," Giannini informed Filippo. "Best Mr. Jefferson did for him was to offer to take him and his sister there to Paris to learn quality cooking. But no promise of his own land's been made."

"No, no land," da Prato reiterated, "but James told me if he learned French cooking while he was there, making pastries and such, and then came on back to teach it to someone else, Mr. Jefferson would allow him to buy his own freedom."

"Glad we were allowed to earn ours," Giannini said to Filippo.

"Someday that will be the way all across this area," Filippo said as he poured the men a second glass of wine. He could only hope that his example influenced that decision, and that watching Giannini and da Prato build their own farms could continue to influence other landowners to act in a similar fashion.

With that business sorted, Filippo entered Jefferson's library and found, according to the letter he'd received, all the letters Filippo had written him as well as copies of all the ones Jefferson had sent. Thanks to the interceptors, only one had ever reached Filippo. Reading them now was like reliving the last few years. While he did find references to his commission and the authentic copies of it, none of the papers that still existed mentioned his salary. It would be necessary to continue on to Montpelier and James Madison.

Before he moved on, he admired the hand-operated pasta machine Jefferson had created in order to make the authentic pasta he had been served at Colle. The memory made Filippo smile amid the gloom of that very empty home. In his own way, he, too, missed the memory of Martha. He could see her now, sitting at the harpsichord in the corner, playing elegantly, but also secretly watching her husband's fingers fly across his violin, carefully working to keep the two of them playing in time together. It had been evident to all their friends that she was the true musician in the family. Filippo keenly felt the loss of a life that would never return. She would be missed by all.

In sadness, Filippo departed for Montpelier and found Madison in better spirits. He was naturally happy to attest to the promises made to Filippo by the council, but had no paper evidence, so he suggested Filippo continue deeper into the country, to the new estates set up by former governor Patrick Henry, who had conceived the mission.

Madison requested that Filippo also speak to Henry about an important government matter. As the new country worked on creating a financial footing, an issue arose that split Madison and Henry and needed to be settled for the country to heal its feelings toward England so commerce could thrive. Boycotts on British materials created during the war taught the then-colonists to do without British goods, and the savage treatment some British soldiers inflected on the populace created grudges that would last lifetimes. Many citizens, including men like Henry, proclaimed loudly that there should be a law that prohibited Americans from paying British subjects for any goods, ever. Madison felt this would hinder the new country's ability to succeed.

"He has been so vehement about it in the press," Madison said, "I did not think it possible to make him retract it."

"Then how can I help?" Filippo asked.

"I believe your experience abroad will help him understand that this is how countries work," Madison said, almost formulating the plan in his head as he spoke. "He has no such experience. And then your skills as a negotiator and your ability to debate… If it is at all possible, you are the only one who can persuade him."

"Then I will go at once," Filippo said. "Perhaps I can solve both our problems with one visit."

"Perhaps?" questioned Madison. "There is no 'haps about it."

～

When Filippo reached Henry's home, he found his old friend had also lost a wife and, out of grief, abandoned the residence they had shared. After two years, Henry had remarried, an event Filippo hoped would happen for Jefferson as well in time. Henry and his new wife, Dorothea Dandridge, had moved to Leatherwood Plantation, a ten thousand-acre property in Henry County, Virginia.

"Congratulations, my friend," Filippo said as he opened the bottle of wine he had brought from the cellars at Colle. "They named a county for you and you deserve it. You deserve this." Filippo gestured across the view of the fields from the veranda where they sat.

"Sarah deserved it," Henry said quietly. "After all those years of scraping by at that lousy tavern, watching the tobacco fail... watching Sarah die. If I hadn't found Dorothea...well, I don't know how Jefferson is going to manage."

Henry gladly gave Filippo the documentation he needed to press for his promised salary, but hesitated at the conversation about paying British subjects. Filippo responded with the argument he worked up on the ride to Leatherwood.

"You must not confuse the innocent with the guilty. These creditors are merchants and manufacturers who have not only done us no harm, they defended our cause with petitions to the king that sought to terminate hostility."

By Henry's silence, Filippo could see that his friend was thinking deeply about this argument, so he bade him good day and departed, having many other friends to visit on his way back to Albemarle County. Before leaving Europe, he had received a letter from John Adams to present to the state government that declared, "Mr. Mazzei has uniformly discovered in Europe an attachment and zeal for the American Honor and interest, which would have become any native of our country. I wish upon his return he may find it agreeable reception." Between Henry's letters, Jefferson's copies, and this correspondence, Filippo had enough evidence to stake and win his claim.

Between these men and Madison and the young Monroe, Filippo also had the makings of a new group that would meet to debate public issues and promote the principles of liberty. They called themselves the Constitutional Society of 1784 and their main focus was to repair the Articles of Confederation, which granted too many rights to the states and too few to the federal government, hobbling that entity in its ability to do what it was created to do: govern. They met at a central location, Anderson's Tavern in Richmond, to pound out ways to fulfill their mission statement, written by Filippo, which promised "the uneducated portion of the inhabitants has a right to be enlightened and advised"—because he believed that "freedom cannot subsist for long in any country unless the generality of the people are aware of its blessings, and tolerably well acquainted with the principles on which alone it can be supported."

To expand the breadth of ideas presented to the society, Filippo wrote letters to the leading international personalities of Enlightenment thinking in Europe, asking them to join in the discussion. Soon, letters flowed between the American founding fathers and men such as Cesare Beccaria, Florentine philosopher Felice Fontana, biologist Lazzaro Spallanzani, and the French liberal François de La Rochefoucauld, all in service to Filippo's idea of connecting "representatives from diverse backgrounds, but who shared, whether scientists or humanitarians, the will to defend religious freedom, the right to one's own opinions, and a belief in political democracy."

While Filippo reconnected with friends, he received word that Maria and her husband, de Rieux, had sailed to Charleston. The countess had discovered the lie about finances that Mrs. Martin had told, and had begun to treat her daughter-in-law, who was pregnant, badly, so the count felt it best to put his son and Maria on a ship for America, knowing that Filippo would pay the passage. While Filippo felt happy at the thought of seeing Maria again and providing the young couple a new start, the news that she'd had a miscarriage on the ship saddened him. In three sentences he went from looking forward to meeting his first grandchild to mourning its loss.

As Filippo was still reorganizing his finances after being gone so long, the best he could do was put up the young couple at Colle while he occupied an extra home of Jefferson's nearby. No one could yet occupy Monticello as Martha's loss permeated the place, making it far too somber and sad for a home for two young people, especially for Maria, who had loved Martha as an aunt. Living at Colle allowed de Rieux to watch over Filippo's crops and Filippo allowed him a patch of land to grow his own for profit. He also helped Filippo with purchasing and selling other commodities between the States and Europe. This business led Filippo to understand the new issues of commerce created by the end of the war.

Just as the three of them began to work well together, and Maria came out of the fog of grief she had felt since the miscarriage, disturbing news came to interrupt their peace: Mrs. Martin was making an unwanted reappearance. Filippo learned that in an escalation of her misrepresentation of their relationship, she had lied to a sea captain, claiming she needed to join her husband and he would pay her passage when she arrived. But the letter she had sent ahead to Filippo accused him of lack of support and demanded a court appearance to present her case.

"I apologize for my mother's behavior," Maria said to Filippo. "You have been ever so generous to me—to us." She reached out to caress de Rieux's hand. "I am deeply sorry for all that she has put you through."

"It is not your behavior and so there is no need for you to apologize," Filippo assured her. "Your father was a good man and his daughter deserves her chance at life."

"What shall you do?" de Rieux asked.

"Pay the man for her passage, as he did it as a favor to me," Filippo said. "But then I will go to a lawyer and have him write up the arrangement we have had all these years, so that if she breaks it again, I will have standing."

Maria offered to stand witness to the full story, which shocked her husband until she explained how Filippo had assigned her mother a portion of the profits from his London shop all those years ago, how she was still receiving that portion annually while Filippo continued to pay for her clothing and housing—as well as Maria's education, and now, her and her husband's upkeep. The couple promised to testify on Filippo's behalf, though he declined their offer. A sufficient number of Filippo's friends and associates on both continents had found Mrs. Martin utterly lacking as both a mother and a wife.

Once this had all been aired in court, the judge found for Filippo. The many, many lies uncovered in the case resulted in Mrs. Martin not being received in any of the homes of her former friends and neighbors. In the end, Maria had to accept her into Colle—for no matter the truth about her, she was still Maria's mother.

With this decision, with a need to reconnect with several business associates in Europe, and with a desire to spend more time with Jefferson during his ministry in Paris, Filippo made plans to return to Europe. He left de Rieux in charge of all the planting at both plantations, with Giannini as head gardener. The soonest ship on which he could book passage was leaving out of New York in two months, so Filippo decided to visit other friends who might join the Constitutional Society and contribute to its mission.

At Mount Vernon he shared lunch with Washington and the conversation revolved around their mutual admiration of the Marquis de Lafayette.

"How I wish he were here to share in the bounty he helped us bring to our countrymen," Washington said in a toast to the Frenchman he had treated like his own son during the conflict.

"Did you know he once told me that we have King George's brother to thank for Lafayette's interest in our fledgling country?" Filippo asked the retired general, who shook his head.

"He never said as much," Washington replied in his taciturn way.

"Perhaps he feared being considered a spy, or you did not talk with him over as much wine as we shared. But Lafayette told me he sat at dinner once with the duke, who hated his brother George III for condemning his choice of a bride. The duke spent the evening praising our soldiers at Lexington and Concord, and somehow that inspired our young friend."

"Whatever it took to bring a man of that caliber to our side, I'm grateful," Washington concluded.

He rushed Filippo through their cigars so that he could show him the kennels where he housed the seven large French hounds Lafayette had sent Washington as gifts.

"All the way across the Atlantic," Washington said wistfully, and Filippo realized that for all his own travels back and forth across the ocean, and for all the other men he knew who had seen London and Paris and beyond in service to the new government, Washington had been too involved leading the army to leave the country on business or pleasure.

"You should go someday," Filippo encouraged his friend. "You would be feted by many."

"Maybe not so many as you think," said Washington in his typical brooding manner. "Besides, my nephew managed Mount Vernon so poorly while I was away, it has required all my attention to put it right. So instead, I will take my pleasure from this home, and these marvelous animals. They are so sweet-tempered and independent. Would that I could say the same of some of our friends."

Washington went on to tell Filippo all his plans to breed the French canines with a pack of black-and-tan English foxhounds that had been given to him by his patron, Lord Fairfax, to create a truly American breed.

From Mount Vernon, Filippo went to Maryland, where a priest from the Carrol family was preparing to go to Europe to take on holy orders. While most Catholics in the United States still resided in that area, some were moving to other states and the Carrols thought a bishop was needed in America to ordain priests locally. Filippo promised to bring up the idea with the papal nuncio in Paris when he saw him during his stay in Europe.

A six-seated stagecoach took Filippo to New York. Where he had once been a prisoner, now he was welcomed by two of the congressional representatives from his home state who also happened to be dear friends and neighbors, Madison and Monroe. They invited him to attend each daily session of Congress, which he did by day, and each night the three of them dined together and debated the decisions coming to a vote the next day.

"The most beautiful thing I have witnessed so far," Filippo said one evening over hot chocolate, "is that everyone values everyone else's opinion and respects the merits of those who hold contrary views."

"Would that it will hold that way," said Madison thoughtfully. "We have deep philosophical divides among the members of this Congress and I don't know what to expect when it comes to handling issues where there can be no middle ground."

"He means slavery," Monroe added. "You can't have half a slave."

"People are beginning to see the light," Madison said. "Several planters have begun the process of emancipation."

Filippo nodded. "Yes, when I was with Franklin in Philadelphia, we stopped in at a laundry he patronized, specifically because the owner, John Payne, had been a planter over in Goochland County."

"I've heard of him," Monroe said. "A Quaker, correct?"

"Yes," said Filippo. "His religion does not condone men owning men, but until Virginia's manumission law, no one could afford to free their people en masse."

"So how is this Payne doing without slave labor?" Madison asked.

Filippo did not want to lie, but he did want the idea of freeing one's slaves to sink in with his two dear southern friends, so he committed the sin of omission. "With clients such as Franklin, how can he not succeed?"

Both Madison and Monroe maintained looks of doubt about the possibility.

"I had a letter from Franklin the other day," Madison said. "He has been told by several friends in Paris that when Jefferson arrived to assume his duties, he was often called 'Franklin's replacement.'"

"Being the diplomat he is, can you guess Jefferson's response?" Monroe asked Filippo.

"Yes," said Filippo, "and I would imagine it would be my response as well."

In unison, all three men raised their glasses to a toast and recited: "No one can replace Dr. Franklin!"

"Yet the two share similar temperaments," Filippo said. "They both enjoy wine…"

"And women," Madison added.

"And they have both already tired of the machinations of our friend in Massachusetts," Monroe said.

"Ah, yes, John Adams," said Madison. "That devout Puritan…he detests Franklin's morals."

"But appreciates his results," Filippo pointed out.

Then Filippo moved the conversation to the other business he needed to do with his friends in New York—assigning power of attorney to Edmund Randolph, John Blair, and James Monroe, who were to settle any business affairs in Virginia and New York while he was in Europe. Madison still couldn't believe Filippo was leaving at such a critical time in the country's growth.

"These Articles of Confederation are failing," Madison stated vehemently.

"We gave ourselves far too little power," Monroe complained. "And we gave the states far too much. Why, they can't even be compelled to pay taxes, yet they demand the use of the federal army whenever Indians attack."

"Our Constitutional Society will handle those questions and present them to Congress in a way that makes change possible," Filippo replied.

"With both you and Jefferson gone, Virginia loses much of her voice," Madison said.

"We will be contributing our support from our position in Europe, but Jefferson and I are already of the past," Filippo said. "You gentlemen are the future. It belongs to you. Take it."

"So you really are going?" Madison asked.

"Though I am filled with a sincere longing to remain in America," Filippo said, "I am leaving, but my heart remains… America is my Jupiter, Virginia my Venus. When I think over what I felt when I crossed the Potomac, I am ashamed of my weakness. I do not know what will happen when I lose sight of its shores. I know well that wherever I shall be, and under whatever circumstances, I will never relent my efforts toward the welfare of my adopted country."

Chapter Seventeen

WITH JEFFERSON IN EUROPE

On June 16, 1785, Filippo boarded a ship bound for Europe along with twenty-two other passengers and a crew of six officers, including the captain. In ten days they made landing in Newfoundland, Canada, and Filippo transferred to a vessel headed for France. Fourteen days later he was dining at the port in Lorient, and arrived in Paris after two days of land travel. While he had old friends in the towns along the route, he hurried to Paris to spend as much time with Jefferson as possible, having heard that his friend still grieved over the loss of his dear Martha.

On their second night dining together, Jefferson found himself sharing his correspondence. Some came from their friends in the United States, some from diplomats around Europe. As he opened the letters, Jefferson tried to focus on those involving business and avoid those still offering condolences for his loss.

He held one business letter out to Filippo. By the wax mark, Filippo could see it came from the office of Elénor-François-Élie, the French ambassador to America.

"François frustrates me the most," Jefferson said.

"But why?" Filippo asked. "I thought losing the French and Indian War had subdued his lust for power, that he was much more congenial now, more open to compromise."

"Failure will do that to a man," Jefferson said quietly, perhaps thinking of the financial strain this appointment caused him. Being away from Monticello meant he couldn't manage operations on a daily basis and wouldn't even hear about problems until they had gone too far to solve. Also, running the embassy cost him quite a bit as the Congress did not see its way to fitting out the establishment in a manner customary to European delicacy. So Jefferson had paid for much of the food and the finery necessary for entertaining diplomats.

"Among other things, I do not understand why a minister of foreign powers makes a mystery out of entirely trivial matters," said Jefferson, waving François' letter.

"That's true." Filippo sympathized with Jefferson's difficult task. "I have found diplomats always padlock their lips, but if you take the padlock off you'll see the trunk is often empty." Changing the subject, he continued, "What of our other friends? What news do Madison and Monroe send?"

"They, too, relish the change you brought to Patrick Henry's position, and tell me business is moving forward with several large concerns in Britain," Jefferson said as he opened Madison's letter. "What's your opinion of our next generation of Americans?"

"Many of our men well along in years and of great worth…" Filippo began.

"You speak of Dr. Franklin," Jefferson teased.

"Among others," Filippo answered slowly and diplomatically as he considered he question thoroughly. "Madison is the youngest, yet no one is listened to with greater attention. We have him to thank for turning the Constitutional Society into the Constitutional Convention—and finally giving us a document that can last."

Filippo could see Jefferson weighing the idea. The new constitution did what Filippo, Franklin, and others wanted by giving more power to the federal government than to the states, but that was not what men of southern birth like Jefferson wanted.

"As much as I admire Madison," Jefferson said, "he may have handed the northern states power to control his financial destiny."

"You know how I have always felt about enforced labor," Filippo said gently.

"It shall pass," Jefferson said slowly, still wondering how.

Filippo turned the conversation back to issues on which they both agreed. "The time I spent at New York watching our young friends in Congress, and then joining them and furthering the debate over dinner. Outside of our dinners here and at Monticello, that was among the happiest periods of my life."

Filippo could see the veil of sadness come back over Jefferson's face as he spoke. "I fear I will never be in such a happy period again, as I was…"

"Martha was a wonderful woman," Filippo said. "One could only pray to one day know such love inside a marriage. You were blessed to be with her for as long as the Lord granted."

"Would that you had been granted such a helpmate in life," Jefferson said, coming out of his reverie to consider the situation of his friend.

The next day Filippo received a letter that changed the course of his travels. The letter announced the death of his brother Jacopo and that he had left everything to his own wife. But Filippo believed their sister, Vittoria, deserved a significant amount to pay her back for her stolen dowry and all the years she had to live with Jacopo, and that he himself deserved the monies his brother cheated him out of years earlier. When he told Jefferson he needed to return to Italy to handle these matters, Jefferson decided to make a state visit himself.

"You know I've always wanted to see your home country," Jefferson said. "And what better way for my Italian counterparts to come to know me than through you?"

The two friends departed together soon after. With Jefferson's retinue managing the travel, it was by far the smoothest move Filippo had ever made across the continent. While in Italy, Filippo took Jefferson to some rice fields as they were both interested in how the crop could provide a better yield in the southern states. Rice had been grown in South Carolina for nearly a hundred years, but Jefferson hoped to add it to the crops at Monticello. He made drawings of the machines the Italians used to clean their rice, and despite the threat of death for violating such a ban, he smuggled rice off the estates in the pockets of his coats. Since olive production also captured Jefferson's attention, Filippo took him to several pressings and together they wrote letters back to Monroe and Madison recommending their cultivation across the lower South.

Jefferson being Jefferson, he and Filippo found time to see the work of the great artists in the churches and museums of the day. Filippo's pride flowed as he showed his most esteemed and elegant friend how his home country appreciated art so much it had started the first art museum in the world. Pope Sixtus IV opened the Musei Capitolini in Rome in 1471 long before Pope Julius II opened the Vatican Collections to the public in 1506.

"We have had museums here before the English even thought of the idea," Filippo said proudly.

But Jefferson was most taken by the art collection of the Uffizi Gallery in Florence. Begun in the fifteenth century by Cosimo de' Medici, it had been enlarged by his descendants, and in 1743 bequeathed by the last heir of the House of Medici "to the people of Tuscany and to all nations." With Filippo acting as Jefferson's agent to the grand duke, who officially owned all the works, Jefferson purchased portraits of European explorers he felt were important to the American narrative, including Vespucci, Columbus, Magellan, and Cortés, and had them shipped directly back to Monticello. Filippo hoped they would help change the feel of the home before Jefferson returned, adding something new amid all the other beautiful things that brought on memories of Martha.

Meanwhile, Filippo had to ask his old friend the Grand Duke Leopold the favor of overseeing the distribution of Jacopo's estate. This became a much more delicate matter when Filippo learned that a friend of Leopold's—a man named Mr. Amburgo, who had several children from his first marriage—was courting his now-widowed sister-in-law. They had registered the intention of marriage within the month. Jacopo had written his will such that if Jacopo's wife remarried, all of her inheritance would go to Santa Maria Nuova Hospital, leaving her penniless. As the man courting her had a title, but no tangible monies to his name, this would be disastrous for their married life. It took all of Filippo's skill and tact to talk the grand duke into assisting.

"But Amburgo is a good man," promised the duke.

"He may be, but his actions will be disastrous to them both," Filippo said gently, knowing how much Leopold liked Amburgo.

"If I cannot stop the marriage, I can ask the hospital to renounce their claims to the inheritance," the duke decided.

Filippo still felt the marriage was doomed, but knew this was the best offer he could expect.

With their business completed, Filippo and Jefferson headed back to Paris. Filippo wanted to stop off in Amsterdam to engage in new business ventures with the Staphorst brothers, but Jefferson longed for the cooking of James Hemings, and so they separated for a while.

On his return to Paris, Filippo visited Haüy at his school for the blind. Haüy was sitting at the end of a very long room where a large number of blind students were absorbed in the new subjects of printing and geography. When he saw Filippo enter, Haüy came at once to embrace him and then called the children to the front.

"My children," Haüy began, "you are not fortunate enough to be able to see him, but call this gentleman, Mr. Filippo Mazzei, your benefactor—for without him, I should never been able to do what I am doing for you."

The children cheered and gathered around Filippo, feeling the fabric of his coat, the leather of his boots, and the writing calluses on his hand. One stepped right in front of Filippo and asked to feel his face, to know him better. Haüy began to reprimand the child, but Filippo stopped him.

"It is a fine compliment this young man is paying me," Filippo said. He bent down so his face would be closer and allowed the young boy to run his hands gently over the contours of his face, feeling his eyebrows, eyelashes, and the slight stubble on his cheeks.

Then the children eagerly showed Filippo the geographical maps Haüy had made in such a way that by touch the boys could tell him the names of the countries, their location, and the bordering countries. Seeing that this establishment must have cost a great deal, Filippo congratulated Haüy.

"How have you been able to afford it all, my dear friend?" he asked.

Haüy embraced him for the second time that day. "Your worthy friend the Duke de La Rochefoucauld, and others who joined him, made and still make it possible."

A few days later, while Jefferson was at the ambassador's residence, Filippo received a letter from John Blair with the news that Mrs. Martin had died. It made for a delicate dinner as Filippo knew watching someone hear of the death of a spouse would bring Jefferson back to the day he lost Martha, and yet Jefferson also knew Filippo and Mrs. Martin had shared a business arrangement rather than a relationship. Sure enough, that difference kept Jefferson from falling into one of his melancholy moments. Instead, he reread Blair's letter, and when he came to the part where Blair regretted and apologized for not sending Filippo a white handkerchief, the sign of true love between a lady and her lover, he couldn't help but comment.

"That would be enough to prove to what point that woman made herself hated," Jefferson said, "since a man so steeped in sweetness and human kindness could joke under such circumstances."

"I only feel for Maria," Filippo said. "It is hard to lose a mother, no matter her behavior."

Jefferson agreed, and fell back into his melancholy thoughts about losing Martha. By the time the letter had traveled across the ocean, arrangements had been made, and despite the fact that she had lost favor among all her neighbors, her daughter buried Mrs. Martin in the family plot on Monticello.

To occupy his time between business meetings, and to continue his support for the Constitutional Society, Filippo took up a task Jefferson had let fall fallow. A new seven-volume book, published by Abbot Raynal, purported to tell all the real news of the European settlements in North America, but those who had actually traveled to the United States found it riddled with mistakes. Some seemed due to ignorance, but others seemed calculated to harm business opportunities between the countries, already so fragile. Jefferson had promised to write a refutation of the book, but had yet to find the time or the inclination. He preferred to focus only on Virginia, creating his *Notes on Virginia* in response, but that left the rest of the new country misrepresented across Europe.

"Writing seems to be our most potent weapon," Filippo said as he agreed to take up the task.

"Ours," agreed Jefferson, "and Lafayette's."

The two friends drank a toast to the other immigrant compatriot of the Revolution. Inspired by the ideals of the American Revolution, Lafayette had recently co-authored the *Declaration of the Rights of Man and the Citizen*, which was adopted by the French National Assembly on August 27, 1789.

Filippo matched the toast. "Not bad company to share at all."

To refute a book that encompassed seven volumes, Filippo required a four-volume set, so many were the misrepresentations he found. When the book *Historical and Political Research on the United States of North America* went to the press for the long process of being typeset and printed, he had time to entertain friends in either his residence or at the ambassador's residence if Jefferson wanted to make their deeper acquaintance as well. Now that the two men were known to be widowers, there was no end to the number of eligible women—widows or potential first-time brides—who obtained letters of introduction or invitations to dine with Jefferson, so he was not always free. In fact, the Italian-English artist Maria Cosway was among the most frequent female guests. She and her husband, Richard, often accompanied Jefferson to art exhibitions around the city. Rumors started about the ambassador and the artist, but Filippo quashed them whenever they came up. Being so close to Jefferson, he knew that his friend still mourned Martha, and his youngest daughter who had recently died. Filippo knew no one could take their place in Jefferson's life at this time.

Among the many interesting women Filippo encountered, he found Princess Marshal Izabela Lubomirska of Poland most fascinating. A cousin to the current king of Poland, Stanislas Poniatowski, Lubomirska had been traveling in Italy and enjoyed engaging in the language with a native speaker. Her travels made her involvement in both political and cultural activities known throughout Europe. For her love of architecture and ancestry she rebuilt the family castle in Łańcut, gathered art collections and libraries, and laid the foundation stone of the National Theatre in Warsaw. She often came to visit Filippo with his new friend, Jean-Antoine Gauvin Gallois, poet of *The Return of the Golden Age* and translator of Filangieri's *The Science of Legislation*. All these blended interests helped enrich the conversation around the table when they visited. Through this friendship with Lubomirska, Filippo met and befriended King Stanislas' secretary, who made an offer to Filippo filled with the most interesting possibilities.

Diplomatic relations between France and Poland had been severed since France had been unable to prevent Stanislas's election to the Polish throne; they disliked him as he was the former lover of Empress Catherine II and therefore the Russian-backed candidate. When the empress then demanded that Poland protect the rights of the country's Protestant and Orthodox Catholic minorities, Filippo knew that if Poland relied on such outside protection, it would lose its independence and France would lose its influence in the area. In the diplomatic desert that these events created, both France and Poland recalled their ambassadors, but kept secret representatives in place. Through intermediaries, King Stanislas asked Filippo to become his agent in Paris.

Filippo took the offer straight to Jefferson so they could hash out the ethics of it over dinner at the ambassador's residence. Jefferson approved of the offer, but Filippo remained unsure.

"But if I take a position in service to a monarch," he explained to Jefferson, "won't I incur the displeasure of my countrymen?"

"I think not," Jefferson said slowly, truly thinking through his idea as he expressed it. "King Stanislas is well known—and well liked—in America…and he is the leader of a republic…not a despot like King George at all…and many believe him to be the best citizen of his country, as each of us strives to be."

After further conversations with Jefferson and other friends stationed in Paris, and full consideration of all the benefits and detriments of the position, Filippo accepted. He began posting letters to the king twice a week regarding the situation in France. The king soon decided that Filippo's main mission would be to restart diplomatic relations between France and Poland. When he succeeded, and it was time to appoint a Polish chargé d'affaires, only one member of the king's advisors voted against Filippo, and then only because of a longstanding law that stated a representative of Poland must be Polish. Since the law could not be changed, the simple answer was to ask that particular advisor to absent himself from chambers on the day of the vote, and so he stayed home and Filippo became the first representative of Poland in France, after a lapse of twenty-seven years.

Diplomatic life entailed attending meetings and dinners and socials constantly, always looking for connections to men of like mind from other countries with whom to conduct the affairs of state. It also involved a precise code of behavior based on one's status in the government. Filippo made very sure to follow all the rules impeccably to maintain his reputation as a man of honor. One night when a new ambassador arrived in Paris with his wife, the queen gave a sumptuous dinner in honor of the lady, as etiquette required. Etiquette also required inviting the most important office holders of the court and of the Diplomatic Corps, but no one whose rank was lower than that of minister plenipotentiary. The queen's master of ceremonies saw Jefferson and Filippo at the same event and so he extended a shared invitation. Filippo knew his title did not qualify him to be at that dinner, and when he reminded the master of ceremonies of this fact, the man smiled and said, "Monsieur is meant to be everywhere." It was perhaps the greatest compliment Filippo received in all his years in Europe.

Diplomatic life also required Filippo to entertain all the Poles who came to Paris in the wake of the reopening of political ties. Entertaining included presenting each of these visitors to King Louis XVI, which kept him constantly busy corresponding back and forth with incoming visitors and the king's court to arrange these events.

Issues arose when the French people began asserting their needs to the ruling monarchy. In conversation with King Louis, Filippo found him to be empathetic with their cause. The king felt their reforms were justly demanded and wanted to fulfill them. Voting in France followed class lines so that commoners had one vote while the system allotted two votes to those of the clerical and the nobility classes. To address their concerns, King Louis called a meeting of the Estates General at his palace at Versailles, which ended in disarray. Commoners clearly wanted change while the nobility defended tradition and the king advocated for compromise.

"His queen is not helping him—or her people—at all," Filippo said to Jefferson one night over dinner. "There is not much to be done about one so haughty and arrogant."

"She reminds me of someone else we both once knew," Jefferson said.

"Yes," Filippo said, "but my late wife had not the power to influence a revolution."

"But we did," Jefferson said, clearly in a lighter mood than was typical.

"I had hoped the French learned from us," Filippo said thoughtfully. "I see the people want what we wanted. Louis sees it, too."

"You'd think he would take a lesson from what they helped us do to old King George," Jefferson said.

"George had it easier," Filippo said. "His revolutionaries were across an ocean from his person. Louis' detractors are within arm's reach."

~

Filippo's fear began to play out in the summer of 1789. With the king and queen still ensconced in Versailles, not having a daily view of the heightening of the crisis, a group of Parisian revolutionaries converged on the Bastille, a royal fortress and prison that had come to symbolize the tyranny of monarchs, with the intention of complete destruction of that detestable icon. The military governor of the Bastille, Bernard-René Jordan de Launay, raised both drawbridges, but his troops could not hold back the crowd, armed with whatever weapons they could fashion. In desperation, Launay raised a white flag of surrender. He and his men were taken into custody at the Hotel de Ville. A hastily convened council of revolutionaries planned to place the governor on trial, but the larger mob broke through and dragged the governor away to an even more hastily arranged execution.

Filippo and Jefferson heard all of this and more from their old friend the Marquis de Lafayette, who dined with them one night when things had calmed back down for a moment. They knew from reports that he had ridden at the head of a detachment determined to keep the peace, one that eventually escorted the king from Versailles to Paris, where he made the speech of his reign.

"No one who heard could keep from being moved to tears," Lafayette said while puffing slowly on his after-dinner cigar. "At the close, the whole crowd came to their feet shouting, 'Long live the king!'"

"I saw a bit of him driving back from the speech," Jefferson told Lafayette.

"I could see nothing at the head of the procession," Lafayette admitted.

"His carriage passed no more than twelve yards from the window of my room," Filippo contributed. "Both ways."

"And what did you see?" asked Lafayette curiously.

Filippo thought for a moment. "On the way in, the king's countenance showed an honest bit of uncertainty, but on the way back, after that speech, with the cannons roaring approval all over town, I believe he felt a great tranquility."

"We'll see how long it lasts," said Lafayette thoughtfully. "We Frenchmen are notoriously high tempered."

"We know," Filippo and Jefferson said in unison.

Filippo continued, "I'm afraid we also know, or at least we feel, some of Louis' troubles come directly from his funding our fight for independence."

"I've heard the shouting at the shops," Jefferson said.

"The king needs to understand the desperation that overcomes a parent who cannot feed their child," Filippo said, remembering his grandfather and all the loaves he gave to the poor. "It is a hard lesson to learn when his son has so much."

"And from our own revolution, did he not learn that overburdening the poor with taxes is the beginning of revolution?" Jefferson added.

"He will not listen to such talk," Lafayette said. "I have tried."

"If he does not hear, he will not survive," Filippo said. "I saw a man ram his sword into the carriage as it passed my window."

"He missed," Lafayette said.

"Others might not," Filippo said gently.

Chapter Eighteen

ALONE IN EUROPE ON THE EVE OF CHANGE

As a representative of Poland during these uncertain times, Filippo was called by duty to visit the court at Versailles and take the temperature of those he met, then make a written report to King Stanislas. Diplomacy required the reading of people, their body language, and the subtleties of their word choices to understand the movement of power. He attended several celebratory banquets at the palace, one attended by the king and queen themselves, along with their nine-year-old son, Louis Joseph XVII, clearly to show him off and remind their subjects of the tradition of monarchy in France. All seemed well enough until the members of the royal family retired for the evening and the banquet continued.

One captain jumped on a table insisting all soldiers present take an oath of loyalty, but his sergeant joined him on the tabletop with another call to arms. "Captain, it is true. We have always obeyed you, and we will continue to obey you when you command us for the good of our country, but not when you order us to go against our own people."

Rather than assuage the sergeant's concerns, the captain had him immediately arrested and that news traveled from Versailles to Paris within the day. By evening, mobs marched toward the palace. The king called Lafayette and his national guard back into service to protect his entourage as they returned to Paris. Other Versailles guests, including Filippo, followed behind the king's coaches.

At dinner that night with the Countess of Albany and her guests, Filippo heard many of them blaming the troubles on the queen. While he did not personally approve of her ostentatious ways, and she did remind him a bit too much of Mrs. Martin, he also knew she had no real power in the government.

"How can you lay blame at the feet of a person who has made no laws, nor made any choices in how the government behaves?" he asked the group. "It was not she who chose to loan my country so much money for our revolution, which, truth be told, was less to ensure our freedom than to continue to plague the English."

"My dear Filippo," the countess began, "in all your time in this country have you not noticed that style is all to us French? Symbolism? Metaphor? And that woman, though she is my queen, is showing the world that all we do is flaunt and flounce while her own people live in fear for their families and futures."

"She only shows the world what her people report of her," Filippo said. "Why are so many taking out their anger at the king and his choices on she who has no choice, not even when it came to her marriage. It seems to me jealousy, as always, is at the heart of who is receiving the brunt of the blame."

An artist among the group grumbled, "As long as she is alive, there will be no peace in the kingdom."

The countess looked to Filippo. "Is that not the ranting of a mad artist?"

Filippo thought for a moment. "While it is certain that painters and poets have a slight touch of madness, they have also a touch of the prophetic. And so I agree, for many reasons. It will not end well."

"No, it will not end well," Jefferson told Filippo the next day at dinner. He had just been recalled to the United States to serve as the first president's first secretary of state and had to pack quickly and arrange passage home. "I wish I could stay and see this through."

"Our country calls for your service again," Filippo said. "It is an honor."

"I think I've been honored enough in my lifetime," Jefferson responded. "I once promised Martha I was done with governing...."

Filippo could tell it wasn't returning to the work of government that bothered Jefferson, but rather returning to a Monticello without Martha that weighed on him. Yet Filippo also guessed that Jefferson was not without love in his life anymore. Before he departed, he told Filippo about a deal he had struck with Martha's former handmaid, Sally, who had served him these last years in France and who all from Albemarle County knew was the half-sister of his beloved Martha. The two women bore a striking resemblance. Filippo had known many a man who, after losing a wife, wed her younger sister. But he also knew, living in the world of legal slavery, that outcome would never be possible for Jefferson and Sally. In fact, Filippo had expected Sally to stay behind in France, where slavery had been abolished, and work in her brother James's pastry shop, living as a free woman. She might even be able to pass as a white woman eventually, since she only had one-eighth African blood.

Instead, Jefferson explained, Sally struck a bargain with him. She would give up her French freedom and return with Jefferson to Virginia if he would promise to free her children when they reached the age of twenty-one, during which time they, like James, would be given an apprenticeship so they could support themselves in freedom.

Jefferson delivered this news to Filippo and to his daughter Martha and his secretary, William Short, over that same dinner. "I want you to know so that, should I not live beyond their twenty-first years, you will make my promise a reality."

Overjoyed at the news, Martha hugged her father, a rare occurrence in their more proper, English-style parental relationship. Living and being educated in Paris had done Martha well, and by living in the ambassador's home she had engaged with world leaders and learned, among other things, that there were countries that had made slavery illegal.

"I wish with all my soul that the poor Negroes were all freed," she said that night.

Filippo felt gratified as the conversation turned to talk of plans to set up their slaves as free tenant farmers when they returned to Virginia. As he had hoped many times before, perhaps his example had finally taken hold. But he also noticed that the seventeen-year-old Martha listened eagerly to William Short for another reason.

When the two younger people had left the dinner, with Short returning to answering correspondence for the ambassador and Martha retiring for the evening, Jefferson told Filippo the final reason he had decided to return to America.

"Martha fancies herself in love with him," Jefferson said, gesturing to the side office where Short had gone to work.

"He's a fine young man—"

"Yes, for a secretary. Not for the inheritor of an estate numbering several thousand acres of prime land."

"I thought in America we had no classes," Filippo gently chided his friend.

"We don't," Jefferson said, half believing and half in jest.

"But Mr. Short has also, to his detriment, shared with me his conquests of several French women here in town. So it is better that Martha and I return to Monticello and let the fires of passion die out."

"And if they don't?" asked Filippo.

His friend had no reply.

The Jeffersons and their entourage left Paris soon after, and Filippo was pleased to receive a letter upon their arrival back home that said Jefferson's promise to Sally had been expanded. He had allowed her brother Robert Hemings to buy his freedom and join an enslaved wife and daughter in Richmond, where they worked for a doctor on the promise of manumitting both women through his salary.

Noting the rising displeasure among the Parisian city dwellers, Filippo helped establish the Club of 1789 and served as secretary of foreign correspondence. The group stated their mission as gathering to discuss and debate current issues to establish union and peace between the classes. Sadly, disagreement arose regarding whether government could limit the freedom of the press, an idea Filippo knew to be wrong from his experiences in the United States. As happens when many men of high station come together, they all want to be heard and they all want their opinion to prevail, even if in private they admit to doubts. The Club of 1789 was no different and this bothered Filippo, but being involved meant he could continue to apprise King Stanislas through mailing him copies of the club's newsletter so that he could decide how to respond, if at all. King Stanislas sided with Filippo in a letter stating, "It seems to me that you have said some very true things to the French people, but I fear the same fate will meet this advice and predictions as met those of Cassandra at the siege of Troy."

Club members often invited other members to dinner or to take chocolate at their homes between meetings so debate could continue. Likewise, members of the National Assembly invited members of the club over to hear their opinions, and on these occasions Filippo felt those men did not understand the danger their country faced.

One night at the home of the renowned chemist Antoine-Laurent de Lavoisier, the one who had differentiated between oxygen and hydrogen, Filippo felt futility finally sinking into his spirit. To try to engage the other guests in the kind of debate that brings change, Filippo said sadly, "I have seen many assemblies, but none so lax as this one in France."

Before any of the other men chose to defend their group, Madame Lavoisier, the former Marie-Anne Pierrette Paulze, spoke in their defense. "Dear Mr. Mazzei, you are doubtless referring to some other assembly than the one on which my husband sits."

Filippo knew Madame Lavoisier to be one of the more intellectual members of this dinner. She played an important part in her husband's scientific career, translating English documents for him to use in research and assisting him in their laboratory. She was not to be taken lightly. But as a woman, she was not a member of the assembly and so obtained her information secondhand, through her husband and his particular bias.

"No, Madame," Filippo responded. "I am speaking of the National Assembly and I repeat what I have said."

None among the men present cared to add to the conversation and it all reminded Filippo sadly of the angels in heaven who chose neither God nor Lucifer in fear of losing their position.

Finally, a short time later, the club approved an idea that would flood France with unbacked currency and, in Filippo's opinion, cause drastic inflation. He resigned and went to Lafayette with his fears for the nation.

"I agree with you, but I can take no action until commanded," Lafayette said.

So Filippo went to the Duke de La Rochefoucauld to see if he could command Lafayette, but the duke did not see the danger in the same way Filippo did.

"We respect your talents and we value your warm heart, but allow us to know our own nation," the duke said. "The rabble have been put down and will not rise again."

No amount of reason from Filippo changed the duke's mind.

"There goes the cause of France," Filippo said. "Each drop of blood you spare now will cost you buckets later."

This feeling of futility, coupled with the absence of Jefferson, caused Filippo to accept the invitation of King Stanislas and travel to Poland. In their correspondence the king had been commenting on Filippo's book and how it explained the lives of Native Americans. In one recent exchange he wrote, "This story will lead us into a theological discussion which I do not wish to undertake by mail, more especially since among the few pleasant things I allow myself to look forward to in this life is the opportunity of knowing you personally."

On the eve of Filippo's departure from Paris, he exchanged his currency at a loss, but once the French Revolution intensified, he would have lost it all, so in the end it was a smart move. In December of 1792, he traveled through Strassberg, Frankfurt, Leipsic, and Dresden, Germany, with Count John Potocki, cousin to the king. At the Polish border, their carriage overturned and Filippo recognized his own symptoms of concussion. Rather than stay at the home of a local lord, as the count suggested, Filippo chose to rush to Warsaw for better hospital care, and so their carriage horses covered two hundred miles in just over twenty-two hours.

The bruise caused by the concussion required Filippo to keep the left side of his face bandaged, even his eye, for the initial weeks of his being presented at court to all the noblemen and government leaders.

"I do believe this misfortune has predisposed people in my favor," he admitted to the king one day at lunch.

They dined together whenever the king's schedule made it possible, and it was always convenient as the king provided Filippo with a large apartment near the palace, a coachman, a cook, and a large quantity of Polish-made products, including a fur robe, a copy of the one worn by the king. It was the most luxurious time in Filippo's life, yet at the age of sixty-two, an age when Franklin had been fomenting rebellion, Filippo felt emptier than ever. And thoughts of Franklin made him sad as well, since the world had lost that wizened man only a year before. As he had always done when faced with sadness in his personal life, Filippo threw himself into his work.

Some Polish noblemen were advocating for playing a similar trick with their currency as the French, and Filippo immediately wrote a pamphlet denouncing the idea. The king had it translated into Polish and fourteen thousand copies were distributed among the populace. In a week, the tide had turned and the idea failed, to the benefit of the Polish financial structure. Filippo was able to report to the king, "Our remedy has reaped satisfactory results."

Next Filippo tackled the diplomatic issues surrounding the suspected betrayal by the King of Prussia, Frederick William II. Twenty years earlier, Poland had undergone its first partitioning. The instability caused by the Polish Civil War allowed Prussia, Austria, and Russia to invade and claim nearly one-third of their land in areas connected to their individual borders. That land grab caused Poland to revise its educational system and rewrite its constitution, but now, in 1791, it faced further threat of Russian invasion and a second partitioning. Which side the Prussian king would take was of utmost interest to King Stanislas. Filippo shared information he had gained while in France about Prussia's designs on Poland, but several Polish noblemen refused to listen. So did the king.

"The King of Prussia has always been like a guardian angel to us in Poland," King Stanislas insisted. "In the last partition he took the least of all the land taken."

"Yes," agreed Filippo. "But he took land just the same. This attitude so many of your men have toward King Frederick is not from reality. A benign glance from a despot works like an enchantment on the majority of men." He let that sink in to the king's mind before adding the most important point. "I must leave here at once. I do not wish to witness the ruin of Poland after having witnessed that of France."

"Patience and courage have been my watchwords until now, and I shall cling to them," the king declared.

"Your faith outstrips mine," Filippo said. "Yet it is hard to leave a friend so true who has treated me with such kindness."

The king took Filippo's compliment as a promise of his intent to stay on, at least through May 3, when he planned a great feast with fireworks in celebration of the adoption of the new constitution. The Italian Opera Company of Warsaw would sing *Te Deum,* a new production by Giovanni Paisiello, the most respected composer of the era. The Polish friend that Filippo had made in France, Princess Lubomirska, wrote that he must stay as he had not yet been to her estate, Mon Coteau. She enclosed the music sheet for a song Franciszek Karpiński had recently written and dedicated to her, the "Song about the Lord's birth," and promised she would play it on Filippo's first visit.

Sadly, that visit never came. While everyone enjoyed the May 3 event immensely, their great joy quickly dampened. Word came shortly thereafter that Russian troops had entered both Poland and Lithuania. King Stanislas sent two regiments of military men to fight, but it looked hopeless. Even the king began to say, "We survived partitioning once, we can survive it again," but Filippo was not so sure. He solidified his plans to leave Poland.

Filippo spent his last day in Poland alone with the king in the king's villa at Lazienky. In all his life, the two men he felt closest to were not his own brothers, but the brotherhood of friends he had created with Jefferson and Stanislas, one a secretary of state and one now a nearly defeated king. He dreaded losing either of them, and to that end, advised the king to abdicate before being assassinated.

"In such an event, dear friend," the king said to Filippo over cigars, "I know of only two cities which could suit me, London or Rome."

"Rome," Filippo said without hesitation, "for the better climate, for the better lasting of your finances, and for your love of art and culture."

"Yes," the king said slowly. "But on condition that I find you there."

For that reason Filippo decided to go to Italy before returning to Colle. At that time Jefferson was living in the capital, Washington, D.C., and not in Virginia, so there was no hurry. Besides helping the king adjust to his new surroundings, Filippo could arrange for more imports to the States to bolster his own finances, since much of the money the Polish government owed him would now be tied up in Russia, or worthless on the international market.

Filippo left Poland on July 7, 1792, destined for Italy and a future happiness he had given up imagining.

Chapter Nineteen

TRUE LOVE AT LAST

Filippo made a quick trip to Livorno to handle some business with his cousins, Domenico and Vincenzo, and generally enjoy their company. While in town they told him how their widowed sister, Signora Volpe, who had been left bankrupt in the first act of unkindness, was now also blind and being cared for by her youngest daughter. Of her two other daughters, one had married and moved to Pescia, and the other had entered the convent. So Signora Volpe and her daughter made a living by taking in boarders. To help them out, Filippo offered to stay there for a fee higher than their normal charge, and after his move to Pisa, he contributed to her annual income with his own money funneled through her brothers so as not to make her feel indebted to him.

In Pisa, Filippo entertained several Polish visitors as they came through, including General Thaddeus Kosciuszko, who was not only a hero in the recent events in Poland, but of the American Revolution as well. The two had met over dinner at Monticello in 1776, when Kosciuszko had come to offer his military talents to the revolutionaries, read the Declaration of Independence, and desired to meet and congratulate the man who had written it. He came to Pisa unsure of his next move and desiring advice from Filippo.

"I fear Poland is lost," Filippo admitted. "I respect your desire to change her fate, but I have lost the belief that such change is possible. If it were me, I would remove myself to the United States, where our dear friend Jefferson now sits as president and the government has already granted you lands for your devoted service during the Revolution."

"You make it sound so simple," Kosciuszko said over wine.

"It is often simple to solve the problems of others," Filippo said. "That is the job of a diplomat."

"Or a cousin," Kosciuszko said, referring to his knowledge that Filippo was not only aiding Signora Volpe, but had also just arranged to finance a room for his cousin Giuseppina Vuy. She had taken the task that falls to all unmarried or widowed women in Sicily, the caretaking of an elderly parent, but that beloved mother had recently died in her arms, and her brother, in an echo of Jacopo's bad behavior, refused to share his inheritance with her.

Filippo kept busy corresponding with friends back in America and learned many good things about their lives. Fearing Filippo might not return to the States, Giannini wrote with an offer to buy Colle, but Filippo chose not to sell. Elsewhere in the area, Monroe wrote to say he had finally been convinced by Jefferson to settle in Albemarle. Monroe's new plantation, Highland, was but a half day's ride from Monticello and Colle. Filippo returned the correspondence immediately, rejoicing over plans for long conversations over dinners in their waning years. "As Jefferson and I will grow old gardening together, so too will you and young Madison," he wrote. Monroe also wrote good news of Madison. Sharing a rooming house with Aaron Burr, the young man earned an introduction to the newly widowed Dolley Payne and they had begun courting.

The news from elsewhere was not so good. In France, as Filippo warned to no avail, the monarchy had been abolished and Louis was sent to the guillotine for treason in 1793. Marie Antoinette became a widow convicted of treason herself, and on October 16, 1793, she too was executed by guillotine at the age of thirty-seven. In Poland, the third partitioning by Russia engulfed all of the lands, rendering the leaders without a country and forcing King Stanislas to abdicate. Sent into exile in St. Petersburg, Stanislas wrote Filippo that he hoped to be granted a travel pass to Italy. Sadly, after his former lover, Empress Catherine, died, no such permission came. Stanislas became one more friend for Filippo to mourn.

In the midst of this sadness befalling so many of his friends, Filippo almost missed the happiness that arrived in the form of their new maid. Antonia Antoni entered the household to assist Giuseppina, who had begun feeling ill. The young woman, nicknamed Tonina, brought her smile and her sweetness into a home that had fallen into malaise, but Filippo was distracted by a flood of correspondence. Monroe now served as Washington's minister to France, a position that found him often writing Filippo for advice. While this came as a compliment, other matters held more urgency. Across Filippo's lifetime his interest in serving others did not always serve his finances well. He would have done better to stay a planter and vintner at Colle.

Now, as he entered his older years, money still owed him for his services in both Poland and America became more necessary, but even more difficult to extract. In America, Madison was working to see that Filippo finally received what was owed him, which gave Filippo some hope, but now that Poland was no more and King Stanislas was in exile, those funds seemed lost forever. So engrossed was he, Filippo hardly noticed the happenings in his own home. Giuseppina noticed him not noticing and took matters into her own hands.

One typical evening Giuseppina and Tonina were working their needles by firelight as Filippo read to them a letter from Jefferson: "I am having the mouldboard plow I designed tested for the possibility of a patent and of manufacturing the tool here at Monticello for sale. An experience of five years has enabled me to say it answers in practice to what it promises in theory. In addition to offering the least resistance as it is pulled through the soil, it shows a further advantage as it may be made by the coarsest workman, by a process so exact, that its form shall never be varied a single hair's breadth—"

Giuseppina interrupted, "I believe I prefer poetry to plowing. Might you return to Dante later this evening? I'm sure Tonina would learn more of use from his philosophy than from Jefferson's tinkering."

"Oh yes, of course." He reached for his worn copy of Dante on the mantel.

Before he could open it, Giuseppina gestured toward Tonina's embroidery. "See how hard she works? And how well?" She pointed to some new pillow covers on his chair.

Since Giuseppina managed the house and all its needs, Filippo hadn't had time to see Tonina's contributions. Now he looked more closely and admired the attention to detail.

"With focus like that, you can't help but create perfection," Filippo said.

As always, in her shy manner, Tonina looked down at her handiwork as he spoke.

"Like a painter but with threads," he added.

Tonina smiled in a new way at the mention of painters. "Threads are all women are given to make art," she said softly.

"Which is your favorite museum?" Filippo asked eagerly. He found himself suddenly interested in her thoughts on his favorite works.

"I only ever see paintings at church," Tonina said.

"That was true when I was young, too," Filippo said. "And if the priest spoke too long about matters too old for me to understand…"

"I would tell stories to myself," Tonina continued, "about the people and the animals in the painting."

Giuseppina didn't want to interrupt the conversation she had finally managed to start, so she slipped out of the room and headed to bed.

Without realizing it, Filippo and Tonina talked until dawn.

The next day Filippo and Giuseppina had an invitation to visit the gardens of a surgeon Filippo knew from his days at Nuova. As they prepared to leave, Filippo turned to Tonina.

"You know, gardens are the other art women are encouraged to pursue. Why don't you join us today? I think you'd enjoy Signor Unis's gardens."

With a nod of approval from Giuseppina, Tonina added more bread and cheese to the basket she had been preparing for them and followed them to the carriage. She sat beside Giuseppina, who noticed that Filippo kept looking at Tonina while talking to both of them.

During the ride, though the paths were no more or less rocky than on their last trip, Giuseppina began to feel pain in her lower abdomen. On arrival, Filippo asked Unis to examine her, which he did, reporting to all that nothing obvious could be detected.

After lunch the women went for a walk in the garden while the men stayed behind for cigars. Filippo looked deep into his friend's face.

"You are worried about something that didn't worry you before we arrived," Filippo said.

"I did not want to worry the ladies."

"What is your diagnosis?" Filippo said, his early training in bedside manner coming to the fore and allowing him to remain calm.

"Tympanites or ascites," Unis answered in an equally calm and calculated manner. "Or both. But a second opinion could be of use."

"Why? You are one of the foremost physicians in Pisa…and both of those diseases are terminal. What matters which one will take my cousin from me?"

No matter how much Giuseppina—or Tonina—tried to pull him into the conversation, Filippo stayed silent for most of their ride home from lunch.

Finally, Giuseppina spoke, "Do not let Signor Unis frighten you, dear cousin. As a doctor he likes to imagine the most interesting diseases, but I'm sure it's nothing but a bit of indigestion from the undercooked rabbit in their red sauce."

It was several weeks before Filippo could bring himself to tell Giuseppina the truth. By then she had taken to her bed several nights after dinner, always sure it was simply indigestion, and always waited on by Tonina until Giuseppina shooed her away to rest. They tried operations and varying her diet, but the only outcome was the shrinking of Filippo's finances. For this he continued his correspondence while sitting at Giuseppina's bedside day and night. Beside him, when she wasn't doing the cooking and cleaning for Giuseppina, was Tonina.

They were not alone. In Giuseppina's short time in the neighborhood, all the local merchants had experienced her kindness and now they gave it back to her in the form of free food and services as needed. If their businesses were of no use to her, such as Ridolfo del Santo the carriage-maker, they spent time with her, reading and watching over her when Filippo and Tonina were occupied. Of them all, the two most loyal caregivers were Ranieri Cosci, the local upholsterer, and Tonina. At one point when Giuseppina became so ill that all hope of recovery was lost, neither Ranieri nor Tonina would leave her bedside. Filippo forced them to leave long enough to sleep.

"You will need your strength soon," Filippo said to them. "We all will."

As Tonina left, she held onto Filippo's hand for a moment longer than normal. Their pained eyes met and there seemed a promise made without words, but one that would have to wait to be fulfilled.

When they were alone, Giuseppina spoke to Filippo in a faint voice. "Do not be alone when I am gone. Do not mourn too long. You have given me a good life, better than my own brother cared to provide…"

"After all you did for your parents," Filippo said quietly.

"He deserved no one in his life. But you do." She looked toward Tonina's chair, where there was a bit of embroidered fabric left in her place. "And so does she."

Kneeling at Giuseppina's bedside to hear her words, Filippo had his back to the door. "But she is young—she should find someone else," he said.

"I found you," Tonina said from the doorway.

∾

They planned to marry immediately so that Giuseppina could be present, but found they had to wait six months so Jefferson could forward Mrs. Martin's death certificate from Virginia. Though he was low on funds, Filippo gifted Tonina a small dowry before their marriage. And then all things financial began to look up, as if his new wife had breathed new life into his world. The Staphorst brothers sent him some funds from business they had contracted in the past, as did friends in America, and several connections in Poland.

He and Tonina shared a happy first year, capped off by the birth of their first child on July 23, 1798.

On the night their daughter was born, Filippo gathered some of the children of the local shopkeepers and other friends to stand outside Tonina's window and serenade her:

Tu scendi dalle stele, O Re del Cielo
(You come down from the stars, oh King of Heaven)
E vieni in una grotto al freddo al gelo.
(And come into a cave in cold and frost.)
O Bambino, mio Divino, Io ti vedo qui a tremar.
(Sweet child, my divine, I see you tremble.)

Slowly, Filippo joined in:

O Dio Beato! Ah, quanto ti costò l'avermi amato.
(Oh Blessed God! How much it cost you to have loved me)
Ah, quanto ti costò, l'avermi amato.
(Oh, how much it cost you, I loved you.)

He caressed Tonina's face as she rested and fed their baby for the first time. "Listen to the children," he said softly. "They are serenading your new child. Music at birth promises a life of love and fortune."

Filippo and Tonina named the baby Elisabetta, in honor of his mother.

Epilogue

Filippo remained interested in philosophy and gardening, and he and his family actively involved themselves in new ideas in horticulture for the rest of Filippo's life. He was able to afford the upkeep of his homes due to a pension from Tsar Alexander of Russia, who took over all of Poland's debts when it was dissolved in 1802. Though Filippo never returned to his beloved Colle, he continued corresponding with his friends in the United States, with Jefferson being the most prolific writer. The men loved discussing their experiments with crops. Even as Jefferson moved to Washington, D.C., to take over the presidency, his letters were full of requests for Filippo to send him ever more exotic plants to try in his gardens. One letter discussed the theft of some German peach and apricot grafts for trees that Filippo sent in early 1804. Another contained a full list of seeds sent from Pisa to Monticello, including various species of strawberries, Maddalena peaches (called "Breasts of Venus"), six grapevines, Malmsey from Piedmont, thirteen twigs of Smyrna without seeds, early roses, Regina plums, mirabelles, white Imperials, and Royal morsel.

The last official act that Filippo performed for the United States government was an 1805 commission from the

Superintendent of Public Buildings in the administration of President Thomas Jefferson, asking Filippo to hire two sculptors to work on the national Capitol. This work required the seventy-five-year-old Filippo to travel to Rome in July of that year. He used the opportunity to take Elisabetta to school in Florence first, and to visit old friends. While in that city, he met Giovanni Andrei and his student, Giuseppe Franzoni, based on the recommendation of friends, and finding them well suited as sculptors, he hired them for work on the Capitol.

By 1813 it was clear Filippo's age would keep him from undertaking the arduous travel to the United States again, so Filippo wrote a letter asking Jefferson to sell his property in Richmond. The money could not be forwarded to him, however, because the new conflict with England, the War of 1812, made its transference impossible. The final letter the friends exchanged was in 1814.

Filippo's last act of writing was to record his memoirs, though they were not published in full until thirty years after his death. Filippo died peacefully in Pisa on March 19, 1816, nine years before his friends Jefferson and Adams.

When Jefferson heard from Thomas Appleton, the United States consul in Livorno, that Filippo had died, Jefferson responded: "[A]n intimacy of forty years had proved to me his great worth; and a friendship, which had begun in personal acquaintance, was maintained after separation, without abatement, by a constant interchange of letters. His esteem too in this country was very general; his early and zealous cooperation in the establishment of our independence having acquired for him here a great degree of favor."

And he knew Filippo's legacy would surely live on.

About the Author

Rosanne Welch, PhD, serves as Executive Director of Stephens College MFA in TV and Screenwriting. Her television writing credits include *Beverly Hills 90210*, *Picket Fences*, *ABCNEWS: Nightline*, and *Touched by an Angel*. For the Mentoris Project Welch wrote *A Man of Action Saving Liberty: A Novel Based on the Life of Giuseppe Garibaldi* (2020). She has also edited *When Women Wrote Hollywood* (2018), named runner up for the Susan Koppelman in feminist studies by the Popular Culture Association and co-edited *Women in American History: A Social, Political, and Cultural Encyclopedia* (named to both the 2018 Outstanding References Sources List and to the list of Best Historical Materials, by the American Library Association). She wrote *Why The Monkees Matter: Teenagers, Television and American Popular Culture* (2016). Welch serves as Book Reviews editor for *Journal of Screenwriting*; and on the Editorial Board for *California History Journal*. You can find her TEDxCPP talk "The Importance of Having a Female Voice in the Room."

NOW AVAILABLE FROM THE MENTORIS PROJECT

A. P. Giannini—The People's Banker
by Francesca Valente

The Architect Who Changed Our World
A Novel Based on the Life of Andrea Palladio
by Pamela Winfrey

A Boxing Trainer's Journey
A Novel Based on the Life of Angelo Dundee
by Jonathan Brown

Breaking Barriers
A Novel Based on the Life of Laura Bassi
by Jule Selbo

Building Heaven's Ceiling
A Novel Based on the Life of Filippo Brunelleschi
by Joe Cline

Building Wealth
From Shoeshine Boy to Real Estate Magnate
by Robert Barbera

Building Wealth 101
How to Make Your Money Work for You
by Robert Barbera

Christopher Columbus: His Life and Discoveries
by Mario Di Giovanni

Harvesting the American Dream
A Novel Based on the Life of Ernest Gallo
by Karen Richardson

Humble Servant of Truth
A Novel Based on the Life of Thomas Aquinas
by Margaret O'Reilly

Leonardo's Secret
A Novel Based on the Life of Leonardo da Vinci
by Peter David Myers

Little by Little We Won
A Novel Based on the Life of Angela Bambace
by Peg A. Lamphier, PhD

The Making of a Prince
A Novel Based on the Life of Niccolò Machiavelli
by Maurizio Marmorstein

A Man of Action Saving Liberty
A Novel Based on the Life of Giuseppe Garibaldi
by Rosanne Welch, PhD

Marconi and His Muses
A Novel Based on the Life of Guglielmo Marconi
by Pamela Winfrey

No Person Above the Law
A Novel Based on the Life of Judge John J. Sirica
by Cynthia Cooper

Relentless Visionary: Alessandro Volta
by Michael Berick

FUTURE TITLES FROM THE MENTORIS PROJECT

A Biography about Rita Levi-Montalcini
and
Novels Based on the Lives of:
Amerigo Vespucci
Andrea Doria
Antonin Scalia
Antonio Meucci
Buzzie Bavasi
Cesare Beccaria
Father Eusebio Francisco Kino
Federico Fellini
Frank Capra
Guido d'Arezzo
Harry Warren
Leonardo Fibonacci
Maria Gaetana Agnesi
Mario Andretti
Peter Rodino
Pietro Belluschi
Saint Augustine of Hippo
Saint Francis of Assisi
Vince Lombardi

For more information on these titles and
the Mentoris Project, please visit
www.mentorisproject.org

Made in the USA
Las Vegas, NV
20 August 2022

53615448R00152